Sweet Rivalry

Also from K. Bromberg

Sweet Rivalry

By K. Bromberg

1001 Dark Nights

EVIL EYE
CONCEPTS

Sweet Rivalry
By K. Bromberg

1001 Dark Nights

Acknowledgments from the Author

This book is dedicated to my book tribe: the women who keep me motivated to sit down and write, who keep me inspired when I don't feel like writing, and the readers who continually pick up my books on the blind faith that I'm not going to disappoint them. Thank you for your support, your encouragement, and your trust.

-Kristy

Sign up for the 1001 Dark Nights Newsletter
and be entered to win a Tiffany Key necklace.

There's a contest every month!

Go to www.1001DarkNights.com to subscribe.

As a bonus, all subscribers will receive a free
1001 Dark Nights story
The First Night
by Lexi Blake & M.J. Rose

One Thousand and One Dark Nights

Once upon a time, in the future...

I was a student fascinated with stories and learning.
I studied philosophy, poetry, history, the occult, and
the art and science of love and magic. I had a vast
library at my father's home and collected thousands
of volumes of fantastic tales.

I learned all about ancient races and bygone
times. About myths and legends and dreams of all
people through the millennium. And the more I read
the stronger my imagination grew until I discovered
that I was able to travel into the stories... to actually
become part of them.

I wish I could say that I listened to my teacher
and respected my gift, as I ought to have. If I had, I
would not be telling you this tale now.
But I was foolhardy and confused, showing off
with bravery.

One afternoon, curious about the myth of the
Arabian Nights, I traveled back to ancient Persia to
see for myself if it was true that every day Shahryar
(Persian: شهريار, "king") married a new virgin, and then
sent yesterday's wife to be beheaded. It was written
and I had read, that by the time he met Scheherazade,
the vizier's daughter, he'd killed one thousand
women.

Something went wrong with my efforts. I arrived in the midst of the story and somehow exchanged places with Scheherazade – a phenomena that had never occurred before and that still to this day, I cannot explain.

Now I am trapped in that ancient past. I have taken on Scheherazade's life and the only way I can protect myself and stay alive is to do what she did to protect herself and stay alive.

Every night the King calls for me and listens as I spin tales. And when the evening ends and dawn breaks, I stop at a point that leaves him breathless and yearning for more. And so the King spares my life for one more day, so that he might hear the rest of my dark tale.

As soon as I finish a story... I begin a new one... like the one that you, dear reader, have before you now.

Prologue

Harper

13 years prior

With each step I take, my temper burns brighter.

Hmm. I don't think they believe you, Harper.

Step.

Hmm. Can't you make that sound more convincing, Harper?

Another step.

Hmm. Are you sure your facts are right, Harper?

Step.

He's right behind me. I can feel him. I can smell his cologne. I can sense his adrenaline just as hyped as mine is.

But in my head all I can hear is him murmur *hmm* in response to every single point I tried to make during our Master's debate. A school tradition more important to most of us graduate students than the graduation ceremony itself. One I was looking forward to for weeks but now feel like it's the bane of my existence.

Flustered, I shove open the door of the lecture hall, thinking it leads to outside and fresh air—distance from him—but all I'm met with is the stale smell of a connecting classroom in front of me and the sound of his feet behind me.

"Harp—"

"Don't!" I whirl around to face him, the fuse to my temper ignited. "Don't you dare Harper me."

His lips slowly turn up in a lopsided smirk as he narrows his eyes as if he can't figure out why I'm so upset.

Not just upset. *Livid.*

"What would you like me to call you then?"

"Go away." I turn my back to him and begin to pace the room, cursing myself for pushing open the wrong door. Fresh air would have been better. Outside I could have kept walking across campus so he couldn't catch up.

"You want to tell me why you're so pissed off at me?"

"You're an asshole." I toss over my shoulder, knowing that's the nicest I'm going to get with him right now.

"Hmm."

There's that goddamn sound again.

"Stop doing that! You're driving me crazy." I rage as I spin around to see him standing there with humor in his eyes. This isn't funny. Him being an asshole is not funny. "Go away! Stop looking at me like that. I don't want you to—I'm so angry at you that...that..."

"Why would you be angry with me?" The blasé way he asks the question makes my temper bristle even more.

"*Why?* Who the hell do you think you are? Sitting there on that stage and questioning me with that annoying sound every single time I stepped to the podium to speak. During my opening arguments, during my rebuttals, even my closing statements. It was hmm and hmm and hmm. That's all I heard."

"Yeah. So?" he asks as he steps toward me, shoulders squaring and eyes challenging me.

My hands fist and teeth grit. His nonchalance only serves to irk me further. "Get. Out."

"Why? Are you so high and mighty on that throne of yours that you think you can do no wrong?"

His words are a verbal slap to the high of winning the debate despite his constant interjecting hmms. I glare at him, my body vibrating, and throw my hands up. "So that's what this is about? Are you *that* jealous I beat you out for first in class that you and your precious ego decided to sabotage me during the debate? Are you fricking kidding me?"

"This isn't about me and my ego," he says quietly as he takes a step closer to me.

"Yeah, right. Like I said, you're an asshole. Thanks for nothing, Ryder." I hate that I'm hurt when I should have known better. I hate that I cared that he was judging me.

He just looks at me with this expression on his face that I can't quite read but don't think I want to. "After all this time, that's how you want to end this?"

"End what?" *What is he talking about?*

Emotion swims in his eyes but I'm so upset and now confused that we stand feet apart without saying a word. He opens his mouth and then closes it before chuckling a disbelieving laugh. "You know what? Forget it. Forget I even followed you back here to congratulate you on winning. Go Bruins! Yay," he says, the sarcasm thick in his tone as he raises his fist like he's cheering me on before waving his hands at me like he's over me and turns to walk out the door.

"Don't you dare leave!" I shout the words as panic suddenly fills me over the thought of him actually doing just that.

His laugh is louder this time as he stops and turns around, hands shoved in his pockets, shoulders shrugged as if to say *decide*. "Make up your mind, Harp. *Get out. Don't leave.* What's it gonna be?"

That slow, easy tone of his is like the scissors snipping at the final strings of my temper. Tears swim again. "Screw you!"

He tucks his tongue in his cheek and just shakes his head from side to side. And I'm not sure why I'm looking for a fight but he's not giving it to me and that only pisses me off further. "You had no right to question me. None."

"You're goddamn right I did!" He's in front of me in a flash, face a reflection of anger—eyes wide, neck strained, hands fisted— that shocks me. "And I'd do it again in a fucking second, so screw you, Harper. Screw. You."

I stand there, a foot from him, my temper seething, my mind a mess, my emotions scattered a million places. "Ryder…"

"No. *Just no.* You don't get to *Ryder* me either." He steps into me, well within my personal space, and stares so deeply into my eyes that I want to look away but don't dare. I meet him match for match. I'm not backing down. And then suddenly, his expression softens. Changes. "Why don't you see it?"

"See what?"

"You're good, Harper. Fucking brilliant. I've sat here for two years—during our entire graduate program for fuck's sake—hating you and respecting you for that alone. You're stubborn and smart and you know everything and you're irritating. You're goddamn right my ego's bruised but hell, you deserve it. All of it. You deserved the respect of every single person in that auditorium tonight."

"I don't understand what that has to do with what you—"

"Don't you get it? I wanted them to see it too. Not your stage fright. But *you*. Your mind. Your brilliance."

He takes a step back, runs a hand through his hair, squeezes his eyes shut as if he's not getting his point across, and yet all I can do is stare at him slack-jawed and surprised at the words coming out of his mouth.

And while I watch him struggle with whatever it is he's trying to finish explaining, I want to reject what he's saying—his reasons and his praise—but it's all so clear now. How nervous I was, stumbling over words and not articulating my points. Then the *hmms* started and it was him I was fixated on. It was the feeling I was used to—wanting to beat him, prove him wrong—that owned my thoughts as my arguments strengthened and my conviction came through.

The crowd disappeared.

The nerves vanished.

Because he was the one I had focused on and was determined to prove wrong.

Just like I've been doing the past two years.

"Ryder." *Thank you. Why did you do that? I'm sorry.* The thoughts don't manifest themselves into words because when he turns to look at me, I feel like I can't breathe, let alone think.

He takes a step toward me then hesitates, but before I can process anything else, his lips are on mine.

And not just on mine—not just a brush of lips against lips—but I'm talking all in. Hands on my cheeks, tongue licking between my lips, body pressed against mine, groan in the back of his throat, type of *all in.*

I don't react at first. I'm stunned. Flabbergasted, my mind reeling from the anger to the surprise to now this without any warning at all.

This is Ryder.

My rival.

My supporter.

My crush.

The thoughts flicker that this is what I've wanted. But they soon shift to panic. To insecurity I don't kiss well enough. That this is all a joke and I'm the butt of it.

But then *I feel.* Everything. All at once.

And I know this is real.

It's like I can't catch my breath and have too much air all at the same time.

My body is on fire. And not just from his touch but from that burn deep inside that feels like it's exploding and imploding all at once.

So this is what it feels like to really be kissed.

It's a fleeting thought before the sensations, the moment, the emotions, consume me whole. His hands move my face to change the angle of the kiss. His fingertips on the line of my jaw singe my skin. His lips move expertly against mine, and all I can do is feel. All I can do is want.

Thinking isn't an option.

The anger from before has morphed to want. The adrenaline has recharged with desire.

There is no rivalry.

There is no graduation ceremony tomorrow I'm missing to catch my flight.

There is no panic over if I'll ever see him again.

It's just him.

And me.

The scent of his cologne in my nose. The heat of his body against mine. The taste of hunger in his kiss.

Only when his mouth parts from mine and the word "Goddamn" is a desirous groan from his lips, does the world exist again. He leans back, hands still framing my face, thumb rubbing over my bottom lip, eyes searching mine with such an intensity that they cause chills to line my scalp.

"Ryder? You in there? I'm so ready for my night of fun!"

Her voice comes through the door and we both startle back a moment before its handle turns.

"It's not—she's not—we're just friends—"

His eyes are wide but full of apology as I just stare at him, high obliterated, the feeling like I'm the only girl in the world *gone*.

I take another step back as the door opens and everything that is opposite of me stands in the doorway—lips painted, body perfect, bubbly personality—and smiles giddily at him.

Ryder holds a hand up to Ms. Perky in the doorway as he takes a step toward me and I take one back.

I fight the tears that threaten.

Over what I've always wanted and know I can never have.

Over wanting to be just like her and instead being just like me.

Over kissing the boy I've wanted for years and realizing he's just as good as I imagined.

Over knowing tomorrow I'm moving back to New York. To my incredible new job. To start my new life.

"I'm sorry." I shake my head slowly as my throat burns with unshed tears. "Thank you. For tonight—out there. For…for the things you said."

Another step in retreat.

"Harper. Come out with us. Celebrate."

"No." I shake my head again. Take another step back, my pride and dignity riding that fine line of breaking right now. "Thank you."

His eyes swim with emotion and confusion.

Because while he may have kissed me on impulse—riding the adrenaline high of the debate and our fight—I kissed him back because for that slight, fleeting moment, I thought maybe I was who he wanted too.

But I'm not.

"Good-bye, Ryder."

Chapter One

Harper

"Mm—mm—mmm. That is one very fine specimen of a man," the lady behind me murmurs to her friend, emphasizing every word.

"I'd welcome getting a little *beard burn* from him."

"I hear that. And girl, that burn can be other places beside my neck, if you know what I'm saying." They erupt in a fit of laughter that is contagious enough to make my own lips curve into a smile.

The lobby of Century Development is full of professionals milling around. I'm sure there are many fine men in suits for the ladies to look at while we trudge through the security line.

"And that ass. Mm, I bet you could bounce a quarter off of it," the first lady says.

"Damn fine."

That's it. My interest is piqued. Admiring a hot guy is definitely a better way to pass the time than checking my emails on my phone.

Especially if he's garnering that kind of reaction from the women behind me.

It takes me a whole two seconds to spot him. There's not much that I can see of him through the break in the security line in front of me, but it's enough to make me want to see more.

And they were indeed correct. Tailored pants showcase one very fine ass. A crisply starched dress shirt frames a pair of broad shoulders. His dirty blond hair with streaks of gold in it hints at time spent outdoors. From my angle, I can't see his face but can make out that the frames of his glasses are black and he's sporting a full beard that looks sexy as hell but doesn't seem to fit with the rest of the clean-cut package.

But damn what a fine package he is.

God, it feels good to be back in Los Angeles. In the city with its stretched out coastline, endless sunshine, and abundance of ungodly handsome men such as the one front and center.

It's not like New York didn't have hot guys because it did, but there's something unique about California men that I'm drawn to. The touch of sunshine on their skin. The physiques honed by outdoor activities. Their laid-back attitudes. And it's been way too long since I've had the chance to enjoy the sights or company of one.

I continue to stare his way in the hopes of catching another glimpse of all of him, but just when I think he'll turn my way, the line shuffles forward and what little I can see of him is blocked. Impatient for the line to move again, I shift on my feet so I can steal another glance but am met time and time again with the solid back of a navy blue blazer on the man in front of me.

If I have to wait in this line, can't the powers that be at least give me a clear line of sight for something good to look at while I'm here?

Better yet, I'll be here the next few days. I wouldn't lodge a single complaint if Hot Guy were to be the sight that greeted and entertained me during my time in the security line before I head upstairs for a long day crunching numbers.

A step forward. A shift of bodies. Another glimpse of him leaving me to wonder what he does here. Is he a regular with a corner office on the twentieth floor with a view of the city below, or is he like me, just passing through for a few days to get a job done before heading home to his wife and two point five kids?

Scratch that. No wife and kids at home. That ruins my fantasy of him. Nah, I bet he likes to go out after work, have a few drinks, and play the field for a bit before taking someone home with him for the night. Because no doubt, a man as attractive as he is definitely doesn't spend many nights with an empty spot on the bed beside him.

And I bet he's a god in the sack. Has to be. A man can't look like he does and be a fumbling, bumbling idiot who's all hands and has little to no dick. Hot-Suit Guy is a dirty talker who likes to be in control.

I'm certain of it.

Maybe I should volunteer my services to him so I could find out for sure.

Talk about a surefire way to relieve the stress of a long day. *Damn*.

The line shuffles forward and yanks my overactive imagination back to reality. Given more time, I'm sure I could make up some more theories I'd like to prove or disprove about Hot-Suit Guy with the nice ass and sexy beard.

I need help. *Truckloads of it.*

This whole train of thought is a stark reminder of something I'm fully aware of: how long it's been since I've gotten good and off. *And God, how I need to get off.*

But I can't think about sex. Or finding someone to have it with. Not yet. First I need to bust my ass, prove myself to the men in the boardroom upstairs that I can handle a job of this magnitude, that I haven't lost my edge, and be awarded this job I'm here to bid.

While sex might help relax me, it'll also distract me because then I'll only want more.

And winning this bid is undeniably my number one priority. The only *want* I'll allow myself to have. Leaving without winning the contract is not an option.

But once I win it, then I'll reward myself with sex. Mind-blowing sex, in fact. And who knows? Maybe if Hot-Suit Guy is a regular here, I can chat him up in the line over the next few days, make nice with him, and then possibly learn the truths to my assumptions.

Work first. Reward sex next.

That'll give me something to look forward to during the next few days. The ones I can't wait to dive headfirst into that will be an ever-changing combination of stress, exhaustion, strategy, and manipulation. An unscripted dance amongst us bidders while we size each other up, calculate our numbers, and explain to the developer why we're the most valuable candidate for the job.

It's the game I love. The competition I thrive on. My return to the job that I've been desperate to make.

And there'd be no better way to make a statement that Harper Denton is back than to leave this building with the multimillion dollar contract for Meteor Development tucked securely under my arm.

And just like that, as a reward for my positive thinking, when I look up, *there he is,* in full view.

I take in the expensive briefcase, the venti Starbucks, and the expensive watch peeking out from beneath the cuff of his shirt. And just my luck that while I'm afforded a full view of his body, the one thing I'm the most curious about is obscured by his hand holding his cell phone up to his ear: his face.

So instead I drink him in. He really is magnificent. I note his posture and the way he carries his body when he moves forward a few steps. There's an air about him that says he's no-nonsense and in control, powerful, and at the same time he doesn't seem uptight. He has that Southern California professional vibe. I can't put my finger on it but he reminds me of someone I can't quite place. Regardless, a man who can pull off being in control and playful has definite merits.

Like "spank me until my body aches in want, and then make a game of hitting each erogenous zone with his tongue before he'll satisfy that ache he created and let me come" type of merits.

The mind-blowing-sex reward just became even more appealing.

I shift my legs to abate that sweet ache my thoughts of him just sparked and realize how rare it is that the hum in my veins over a man has been rivaled by the thrill I get competing in the boardroom. And for that thought alone, I indulge a bit more in thoughts of him, knowing when I get stressed upstairs, I'll be able to fall back to them.

Use them as an inspiration and a reminder of what I get when I achieve success.

I'm jolted from my ridiculous yet fulfilling fantasy as Navy Blue Blazer Guy accidentally turns and bumps into me. Apologies are exchanged before he lifts his hand in greeting to someone he sees across the lobby and unexpectedly leaves his place in line. I move forward, my gaze naturally landing back on the bearded eye candy now two people in front of me.

"Shouldn't be. No...I'm confident. From what I gather, the project seems pretty straightforward so..."

His voice hits my ears and breaks through my waning patience. And hell if his voice isn't as audibly sexy as his body appears to be. It has a grate to it that sounds like what my wild imagination conjures up is akin to the feel of his hands running over my skin. Rough but smooth. Patient but commanding. A little bit of an edge to it. But it's what he says next that holds my attention more soundly than his overriding sex appeal calling to every ounce of estrogen within my body.

"Seriously. This isn't my first rodeo but it's definitely a new approach. The bid list is being kept private so I'll find out who's competing as soon as I get in there... Dude, you know me. I've talked to people here and there, know some of the names being tossed around. Harry from Meteor was supposed to be a shoo-in, but now I've heard he's gone. Not sure the circumstances but that's a definite plus for us." His laugh that follows is full of arrogance. The sound of it bristles over my skin, washing away that feeling of familiarity that tickles the edges of my mind. I inch closer, my back a little straighter now, and my attention more than piqued. "I know. Yeah. I don't know for sure why but I heard they hired some hotshot fresh from New York, so you know what that means...a glorified assistant straight out of college they're feeding to us wolves who has no goddamn clue what he's doing. Good luck with that, buddy. At least I'll have some entertainment watching that train derail."

I clench my jaw as a person squeezes through the line in front of me, forcing me to lose my concentration momentarily. The line moves forward again, the metal detector in view, and yet my sudden urgency to get upstairs and start has waned. Eavesdropping about my assumed abilities is so much more fun.

"Nah. Nograd's always dead middle. He won't go low enough to take a risk and too high is a death wish. This project is out of his league. The rest are just here so Century Development can say they ran a fair bid when in the end it will come down to the usuals. Like always." He laughs again. "I'll play the game. Don't worry. I'm confident. Yeah. See ya."

My mind stutters over thoughts, eyes focused on the back of his hand holding his phone, with emotions swirling that I never allow to show. A glorified assistant? I bet my track record is more extensive and exclusive than his by a mile.

Prick.

He may be hot, but he's still a prick.

Then again, let him underestimate me. If he's so cocky he thinks he has this in the bag before he even starts, then he deserves what he gets when I beat him handily upstairs.

Screw him and his nice, Starbucks drinking ass.

He'll learn the error of his ways soon enough. I may have purposefully kept my return under the radar, but those in the know will recognize my name once the bid list is revealed. I'm certain a few will even be a little shocked. New York is a long way from Los Angeles, but that doesn't mean they're not familiar with the name Harper Denton or my reputation as a no-nonsense, ball-busting businesswoman not afraid to get her hands dirty to deliver a project under budget and on time.

What a pity he turned out to be an ass. I had so much hope for us.

I smile and sigh. Well, at least I'll have something pretty to look at while I'm working.

Besides, what person is that arrogant that they talk shit about their competitors in the lobby where they're supposed to meet for the bid? Someone is bound to hear him so maybe he's that secure he doesn't care?

I glance Hot-Suit Guy's way just as he lowers his phone and takes his briefcase off the security table. It's when he lifts his face to flash a smile at the security guard with an All-American charm I'm way too familiar with, I freeze.

...no way...

I know him.

...it can't be...

Ryder Rodgers.

Son of a bitch.

I should have known.

And so we meet again.

This is going to be so much fun kicking his ass.

Again.

Chapter Two

Harper

I know the minute he enters the boardroom.

Yes, there are about thirty other men filling the space—my fellow competitors and some Century Development employees—and yet I can *feel* when Ryder walks through the doorway. I know he's there. And without looking up, I can distinguish his laugh as it rumbles through the space and commands the attention of those in the room.

Everyone's attention that is, but mine.

Because I don't care that he's here. Don't care that he seems at ease with the guys, slapping backs and shaking hands like he owns the place. Don't care that his charisma is palpable and pulls on every part of me and begs me to look up.

Ryder Rodgers does *not* command my attention.

Hell, who am I kidding? He commanded my attention years ago and then owned it again in the security line before I even knew it was him.

His laugh rings across the space again and breaks through my thoughts of him, but I refuse to look up and give him any more of my attention. Especially since he's all I've thought about since he walked away from the security station downstairs.

I should be focusing on the task at hand. The bid we're about to start. The game we're about to play that just changed in so many ways for me.

Not thinking about a kiss we shared way back when and wondering if he's ever thought twice about it like I have over the years. Like maybe when his name has been brought up in business conversations.

I should be writing down the names of the competitors in the room. Making a list of them so that I can research them later when I'm alone in my room.

Not wondering if beard burn is a legitimate thing and if so, imagining how damn good it would feel getting it.

Jesus, Harper. Get a grip. Shut him out. It's *just Ryder.*

And therein lies the problem. *It is just Ryder.*

But I've shut him out before. I can do it again. No one knows better than I do how he can take advantage of any distraction to get an edge.

And I can't be giving up any edges. Not now that I know he's here—*just like old times.* I have too much riding on this bid to let Ryder get in the way, and no doubt of all the people in this room, he'll be my biggest challenge.

I wouldn't expect anything less from him.

He laughs again and my body doesn't heed the warnings I've been giving myself because I glance up to where he's chatting up three other competitors.

Now that I can see him from the front, I can affirm one of my theories. He's definitely sexy. Add to that he's changed from the coed I used to know—body filled out, ass definitely tighter, and that beard? Damn him for that. Let's pray he doesn't have tats beneath that crisply starched shirt of his or I may be sending out an SOS.

Then again, why ask to be rescued since the man sure knows how to kiss a girl so it's forever seared into her memory?

Beards, tats, tight asses, and searing kisses? That's a great way to start with your head in the game, Harper.

He glances over my way and I immediately look down, not

wanting him to know I'm here yet. But when I do, I notice that the only competitor I've added to my list on my perfectly white piece of paper is *Ryder Rodgers.*

And right on cue, as if I'm not paying him enough attention, his voice carries across the space and demands my attention.

I don't look.

No doubt he's smarter now, with more experience under his belt.

I won't look.

More polished and professional.

I refuse to give him the satisfaction later of knowing I looked.

Smoother with his tactics and less brash with his decisions.

Dammit, Harper.

My eyes are on him, appreciating not only the sight of him and the way my insides twist because of him, but also the firing of the competitive edge inside of me.

We're going to kill each other. The thought makes me laugh because if our interaction in the past is any indication, it's not far from the truth. And that's why I'm sitting in the back of the room with my head down and letting them assume I'm the glorified secretary from Meteor Development. Because if blood is going to be shed, I might as well draw the first drop and use surprise to my advantage to get it.

No one knows I'm back.

This bid just became so much more than numbers. The want to prove myself just increased tenfold. To the industry that let me down as a whole, and to the boy I had a crush on who never knew.

As if he knew I needed help refocusing on the task at hand, Mason Van Dyken, Century Development's CEO, walks to the front of the room to welcome us. And that's all it takes for that buzz of excitement to overpower every other thought I was having and redirect it to exactly where it needs to be, the project. The numbers. The details of what's to come.

From my vantage point in the back of the room, I listen and take notes. Thoughts of Ryder fade to the background as I ride the high of being back in my element and welcome the firing of my competitive spirit after having suppressed it for so long.

When Van Dyken asks us all to introduce ourselves, the men seated in front of me begin. I recognize the names of competitors I've researched as the introductions continue around the room.

And this time I take notes.

"Brandon Tennison with Nograd."

There's silence as the rest of the room nods in greeting while silently scrutinizing him. The mental warfare has begun.

"Alan Danks with Developmental Solutions."

More silence, more nodding of heads, as the introductions weave through the tables in the room from front to back.

"Ryder Rodgers, R Squared Management."

I fight my own smile over how surreal it is to hear that name right now. And with the anticipation of what his face is going to look like when he realizes I'm not really that glorified assistant he has assumed me to be.

I'm the last person in the room for introductions and when it's my turn to go, I keep my head down while all eyes turn my way. I can feel the weight of their stares as they look at the top of my blonde chignon. I wait a beat, allow them to assume I'm intimidated by this room full of powerhouse men that's causing the pause...being the *assistant* and all.

They couldn't be further from the truth.

And it's going to be so fun rubbing their noses in it. Little do they know I'm not intimidated in the least. I live for this shit— proving those who underestimate me wrong. And the one person who knows that better than anyone in the room is the one this little show is intended for.

Surprise, Ryder. Look who's back.

I clear my throat, slowly lift my face with a slight smile curling the corners of my aptly painted pink lips, and introduce myself.

"Good afternoon, gentlemen. I'm Harper Denton. Meteor Development."

Chapter Three

Ryder

"Mr. Van Dyken," I say as I cross the room and reach my hand out in greeting. There's no way I'm letting Harper carry on her one-on-one conversation with him without stepping in to interrupt.

And damn straight, I want to turn to her, stare at her, and ask her what the hell she's doing here when last I heard she was kicking ass in New York, but I don't give a glance her way. I see her scowl though, know she's pissed I'm cutting into her schmooze time with Mason, but I couldn't care less. She had plenty of time to come up and say hi to me before Van Dyken started his spiel. But *she didn't*.

And why not? Is the game that important to her she can't say hi to an old friend? Typical Harper. She looks like heaven but is still cold as hell.

So she wants to start off like this and set the tone? She better bet that very fine ass of hers I'm going to follow suit. Difference is, this is my turf now so if she wants to play, she's going to have to step into the ring first.

My ring. My rules. Not hers.

I'll even be a gentleman and lift the ropes for her to climb in between.

"Ryder. So glad your company had the wherewithal to send their very best for the job."

Hear that, Harper?

"I wouldn't pass up this opportunity for the world. You have the lot of us on pins and needles waiting to find out why there's so much secrecy over this project. We're all eager to find out the face behind the mask that's pulling the strings."

"In due time," he says with a knowing smile that hints he's enjoying this little power play a bit too much, but he's allowed. He's the one in the know.

"I was excited at the chance for this project given how well we've worked together on projects in the past."

"You definitely know my favorite words, Ryder."

"*On time* and *under budget*," I say as his laugh booms around the room. Heads turn and competitors take note of who he's speaking with.

Exactly my intentions.

"Just what I want to hear. How can I—excuse me one second," he says as he's summoned away by an employee across the room.

"Still great at kissing ass, I see," Harper murmurs the minute he's out of earshot.

And she just stepped into the ring. I didn't doubt she would for a second. Let's see if she wants to play with the gloves on or off.

I turn slowly to face her, the disbelief that she's here still as real as when she lifted her face to meet my eyes with that smirk playing at the corner of her lips like she did earlier in the conference room.

"Still great at being hostile, I see. Hello, Harper." My greeting and smile are a mixture of cautious sincerity. "And after all this time I thought you might have changed. So refreshing to see you haven't."

Ding. Ding. Ding. Round One.

"Hello, Ryder." She gives a subtle lift of her brow as our eyes hold longer than they should. A nonverbal challenge that's welcome and terrifying all at the same time.

"Such a pleasure to see you again."

"Well, at least I know you're still good at telling a lie. We both know you're far from happy I'm here." Her laugh is throaty, her lips distracting.

God, she's gorgeous.

I reject the thought the minute it hits me but how can I fucking argue that she isn't? She's all curves and confidence and sex appeal wrapped in that sophisticated, damn business suit. Her expression may say *drop dead*, but her body screams *make me feel alive*.

"Think what you will. I'm glad to see I still bring out the best in you."

She snorts. It's such a contradiction to the completely put together woman before me and yet the sound of it tells me a bit of the old her I used to know remains. The one from *before*.

"True," she muses nonchalantly, eyes focused on the other side of the room. "I mean look how the last competition ended between us…" The comment is left open-ended but the lift of her eyebrows and purse of her lips say the words for her: I won.

"Good thing I've learned the error of my ways since then."

We hold each other's gazes, our lips fighting back smiles while unspoken challenges war between us.

"I'm sure you have, but we both know you're standing here sizing me up, asking yourself who is this woman who sounds like the Harper Denton you once knew but looks nothing like her and is ten times smarter now…and then you're wondering if your best is enough this time around?" she says, a coy smile on her lips and my own mouth falling lax as she makes her mark and hits the nail directly on the head. She lowers her voice as if she's going to let me in on a little secret. "The answer is no."

She's good. Damn good.

The Ice Queen returns.

I chuckle and shake my head. I shouldn't be surprised that just like that, we're picking up right where we left off. And just as I'm about to speak, her smile widens and tells me that Mason is on his way back.

"Sorry about that. A few details needed clarifying." Mason interrupts as he returns and looks from Harper to me and then back to Harper. It's not hard to sense the tension—competitive and sexual—that always seems to be a constant between us. "You two have met then?"

I nod. "We've competed a time or two in the past," I respond, trying to play nice.

"Hm. I wasn't aware. Sometimes familiarity can be an advantage. *Or a liability.* I'll enjoy being the benefactor of both." He glances between us again, momentarily lost in thought before he rubs his hands together in front of him. "Now, what was it we were discussing?"

"I was just letting Ryder here know what other projects are coming up for bid in the vicinity. I figured it's only kind to give him his options since I'll be winning this one." Harper's smile is sweet and genuine to match the playfulness of her tone and yet I know she means every word.

Mason's laugh rumbles through the room. His quick grin tells me he respects her for having the balls to make the comment. Who doesn't respect a woman making a definitive play in the male-dominated world of construction management?

"We'll see about that." My smile is tight as I meet her eyes, my own warning fired off in the silent exchange.

Mason looks between us again. "This is going to be fun to watch. Nothing like a good, clean fight between colleagues. Excuse me again, but we're going to get the presentation back under way shortly and I need to tend to a few details first."

We both turn to watch him retreat, and I swear I hear Harper mutter under her breath, "Who says I don't like things a little dirty?"

The minute the words register, my mind immediately goes *there.*

To dirty.

And with Harper.

I full-on stare at her to question if I heard her correctly, but her face is the picture of innocence. All but the tiny little quirk of the corner of her mouth that tells me I heard her right, and that she's fighting like hell not to smile.

I've got to give it to her. The woman's got chops.

"*Dirty, huh?*" I can't resist. Challenge accepted. The murmur is off my lips without thought, my body already wanting to find out just *how dirty.*

She clears her throat and gives up the fight, letting her lips spread into a slow, knowing smile. "Wouldn't you like to know…" she says with a glance my way, eyes lit and eyebrows raised before she walks away without another word. Well, unless you count something she mutters that sounds a lot like *fucking beard burn* while leaving me the very fine visual of her hips swaying in her gray pencil skirt and pink heels as her way of driving the suggestion home.

And there is no driving it home needed. Her point was made loud and clear, and with a fuckton of room left there for my imagination to improvise. Like how I'm reliving my grad school fantasies of taking the shy girl with the mesmerizing eyes and intimidating intellect on the desk in the empty classroom, and at the same time dreading the fact she's been invited to bid.

And round one goes to Harper.

Damn. She always did have a way of boiling my blood and getting me hard all at the same time. Seems like she's perfected that skill of hers over the years.

I'm not sure if I should be happy about that or fearful. Fuck if I don't love a strong, confident, intelligent woman. The feistier the better. Talk about sexy as hell. But when it comes to *that self-assured woman* being *Harper*, it means this bid isn't going to be as in the bag as I thought it was going to be an hour ago.

Good thing I like to be challenged.

I lift my bottle of water to my lips and wish it were a beer. I think I might need it or *something stronger.* Can this situation get any more fucked up?

Only if I were to sleep with her.

And with another look over to her, I hate myself for wanting to but can't blame myself all the same.

I haven't felt this conflicted since that last week of school.

Well, shit. *Hello, Harper Denton.* So we meet again, *Ice Queen.*

At least Van Dyken was right about one thing—knowing her can have its advantages.

Like knowing she'll go straight for the jugular without a second thought.

Best to keep that in mind so I don't get caught flatfooted staring at those legs of hers.

Chapter Four

Ryder

High heels.

What the fuck is she doing here?

Bare legs.

And not just here in the office, but in Los Angeles altogether.

Sexy calves.

Wasn't she off in New York conquering the world or something?

Pencil skirt.

Maybe I like it a little dirty.

Shoot me now because the damn view in front of me is enough to distract me from paying attention to Mason as he points to where the facility will be laid out on the land before us.

"...in an unprecedented move, Century Development has changed the way it's doing its bidding process for this project. In lieu of our typical sealed bid, we wanted to control the bidding environment in all aspects of the process..."

I should be turned on by the sight before me: a vast amount of undeveloped land. A rarity in southern California these days. The one thing someone in my career can't wait to get their hands on.

Get dirty in.

Dirty. There's that word again. And of course when I think of getting my hands on something and the term dirty, my eyes veer right back to Harper.

To the curve of her hips. The square of her shoulders. The tight knot of hair at the base of her neck that fits expertly beneath the yellow hard hat on her head, an item every person here no doubt hates wearing in the warm sun, and yet somehow she makes look sexy.

Jesus, Ryder. Remember who she is. Competition. *Sexy competition with sharp claws she won't hesitate to use.*

Not like I ever complained about scratch marks before though.

"…the renditions back at the office you saw before we headed out will be available to you for reference during the bidding process, but I felt it was important to visit the site to see the magnitude of the project in person…"

She's probably doing this on purpose. Wearing the skirt and the heels when she knew we were going to be headed out to a dirt site. Totally impractical. Sexy as sin. Fully distracting.

And I'm losing my mind.

Those heels, though. I laughed when she climbed out of the car with them still on because I was sure as shit that she was going to wobble on the uneven dirt surface. That she was going to pull the I-can't-walk-in-these card, and yet of course she hasn't. But I should know better by now not to underestimate her. She's been nothing but sure-footed. Smooth as silk. Completely competent with both her questions and her spiked heels in this rocky terrain surrounded by men.

It shouldn't surprise me…

Mason continues on, pointing out the approximate locations for the five different buildings that make up the whole of the facility. I listen passively because I've already plotted them in my head from the full-scale renditions we were able to study back at the office.

I glance around to my competition. To Brandon from Nograd, with his Lacoste obsessed wardrobe and his too-tight pants that are so representative of his uptight temperament. He won't bend, isn't good with having to adjust, and is no doubt bursting a blood vessel right now because he doesn't have the rest of the details of the project yet to obsess over.

To Alan from Developmental, with his half-tucked dress shirt and messed up hair, and I know that his socks are probably mismatched—both gray, but definitely with different patterns— because he gets dressed in the dark of his bedroom to let his wife, who works the graveyard shift as a nurse, catch up on her sleep. A good guy but sometimes so distracted by his kids and wanting to be a good dad that he does his math a little too quickly or overlooks a line item and comes in at a number too good to be true and therefore is often disregarded.

To Patrick from Lux, with his slicked back hair and smug smirk that I know rakes in the ladies and yet I want to wipe it off his face because I know after he reels them in, he treats them like shit, and that's unacceptable. But it's representative of how he treats his projects: thrilled to get them but then mishandles them once he does.

There are others around me but I don't bother to study them because they're here simply for the experience. Century needs to prove to whomever they're running this project for that they've gotten the best of the best. And that means having a multitude of qualifying companies compete so they have more numbers to show fairness.

But not Brandon, Alan, or Patrick. I've worked with all of them before. Have bid against them. Have done the mandatory social bullshit required to be a part of the building industry. I know them well enough to know where they'll fall in line with their numbers, what their bosses demand and dictate in a profit margin, and how they react to the unpredictable, such as this situation.

I can read everything about them. That's what I do. I study. I remember. I use it to my advantage when I package my bid together.

And yet when I return my focus to the land before me— Mason talking in the front and Harper just off to my left—I hate that I can't read *her*. I know she's just as important competitively—if not the most important one—and yet her edges seem sharper, her demeanor hardened from what I remember it to be.

I may be a take it as it comes type of guy, but fuck if the unknown isn't unsettling.

"...let's head back to the office now and I'll get you the rest of what you need so you can get started."

There's a murmured consent among all of us as we all follow after him toward the waiting cars. I walk a few feet and then swear at my mother and her inherent need to hammer manners into my head as a little boy. But I listen to her silent voice nonetheless, and even though I have a feeling Harper's going to be pissed I'm calling her out as a woman with the gesture, I turn around to let her pass and go ahead. *Ladies first.*

But just as I turn, I'm met with a small yelp split seconds before Harper's body collides squarely into mine. Already off balance, I stumble backward a few steps the same time as my hands tighten in reflex to prevent her from falling farther.

Seconds feel like minutes. Her hard hat slips off and clatters to the ground when she tilts her head up with eyes wide and lashes fluttering to look up at me.

Our eyes hold. A solid punch of too many things hits me—the heat of her body pressed against mine, how tiny and fragile she seems in my arms when she's always strong and in control, and the flicker of vulnerability that flashes through her eyes.

It's gone just as quickly as I see it but in that second, we're back in the darkened classroom. My lips are still warm from hers, my body reeling from her taste, and she's looking up at me with that mixture of shock, desire, and vulnerability that I was probably too young to understand and too stupid to appreciate at the time. The one that should have led me to chase after her when she ran out the door instead of question the consequences first and never get the chance to later.

But there was more there. I know there was. And right now, the look in her eyes when they meet mine—with the dirt beneath us and the sky above us—brings it all back.

Déjà vu like I've never experienced before.

As quick as the memory comes, it's gone. And I know she must have thought it too because within a beat, we're a sudden mass of hands pushing off, eyes averting, and throats clearing so we can erect that professional wall back between us. I step away and pick up her hard hat while she smoothes her hands down the line of her skirt.

"Are you okay?" I hand her hard hat to her. Watch her throat move with a swallow. See the flush of embarrassment in her cheeks. *Does she think all these same things when she looks at me?*

"I'm fine. Thank you." Her voice is tight, movements determined, as she takes the helmet and strides past me without another word.

Curious yet cautious thoughts start to spin out of control in my own head, that I can't allow myself to think. I turn on my heel to follow her just in time to catch her shrug off the other men asking if she's okay. She strides right past them with a laugh but determination in her gait.

We climb into the waiting town cars ready to bring us back to the office tower and pull out of the dirt lot with a billow of dust around us. She refuses to look my way the entire return trip. And even though Alan's presence in the front seat prevents me from asking more, I have a feeling even if he wasn't here, she'd still refuse to acknowledge what happened.

But my unfinished thoughts prevail. What if I had chased after her that night? How would things have been different, or would they have at all? And when I tell myself what-ifs aren't worth dwelling on, my mind shifts to the look that was in Harper's eyes.

A look similar to the one my three-year-old niece gets when she's hurt or afraid but is trying to pretend like hell she's perfectly fine. *A brave, little girl in this big, bad world.*

Guess Harper's not so sure of her heeled feet in this world after all.

And why does that thought bug the shit out of me?

Chapter Five

Harper

I'm the first in the room, my mind focused on getting to work, my body still reacting to the feel of Ryder's body against mine.

That's what I get for taking a minute to appreciate the sight of his very fine ass walking in front of me. Take my eyes off the dirt for one damn second and I almost fall face-first and make an idiot out of myself.

Correct that. I did make an idiot out of myself with what felt like a million other eyes watching. Ain't that a kicker? Try to prove you're a woman, capable and tough, and end up looking like the helpless damsel.

Of course, no time like the present for the prince who saved me to enter the room. Needing space, I step to the opposite side of the crowd as him because I can still feel my body against his, can still smell the subtle scent of his cologne, and can still see that look in his eyes from earlier today when I don't want to.

And then I'm left to wonder if that fluttering I feel is from today or just the memory of *before*? Which one has my body standing to attention when his undeniable presence is near?

How can one mistake of a kiss years ago still make me feel this way?

Because it was one helluva kiss. *That's why.*

My thoughts are interrupted when a woman hands me a colored file folder with the number "13" and "Harper Denton" written on the front of it.

"Please don't open anything yet," Mason's assistant says as Mason, himself, walks in the room, right as I was about to do just that.

The subtle hum in my veins returns because we're about to get started. The bid, the competition, the fight for first. There's no better feeling than walking into a room as the underdog simply because you're a woman, to later walk out the victor because your skills and expertise proved them all wrong. And because of this—my drive to prove I'm better than my competitors are, that I need to refocus and get myself back on sure-footedness that the dirt dusting my heels tells me I lost today.

I look around to see everyone else with that anticipatory look on their faces, their excitement palpable, and wonder if it's the same for them as it is for me.

"Hey, Harp." Ryder's low timbre is whispered in my ear, his chin hitting my shoulder as he speaks. I freeze, hold in my yelp of surprise that he's behind me when he was across the room a second ago, and try to remain as professional as possible when everything in my body feels like it has just been electrified. "Just in case you were wondering, *beard burn* is a real thing."

His chuckle rumbles from his chest into my back before he steps away. I'm left staring at the number thirteen on my folder and pretending to remain unaffected to the people around us—like he was discussing the particulars of the project—while inside I'm dying a slow, beautifully torturous death of desire.

My mind shifts gears suddenly and realizes he heard me. Actually heard me as I chastised myself for thinking about it while we talked earlier. Can this day get any worse?

But before I can turn any redder, Mason takes charge of the room. "You'll note the full-scale model has been placed in the center of the room to make it easy for you all to see from your seats. Elevation renditions are hanging on the wall to your left and a nonnegotiable construction schedule with deadline dates is hanging on the wall to your right. We've set up a desk for each of you and you'll find it fully stocked with supplies, calculators, etcetera," Mason says with a flutter of his fingers as if all this secrecy is self-explanatory.

We all glance to the two rows of desks set facing each other a mere five feet apart. *Talk about staring down the enemy while you work.* I catch a few furrowed brows of the guys around me as to why all the hubbub and quietly sympathize because I feel the same way.

"By now, each of you should have a file folder in your hands. These are your bibles for this bid. It is your information and yours only. That folder is not to leave this room and it and its contents should remain on the top of your desks when you leave each night."

Expressions become more bewildered. This stipulation means that our bid calculations would be sitting in plain sight for any of our competitors to open and look at if they wanted to see our numbers.

"Doesn't that allow for—"

"I know it's unconventional, Brandon, but it's the way the contractor wants the bid run and therefore we are following through with his wishes. A couple of notes before you begin. The client is very specific in his demands for the project. He will not negotiate with you over your numbers, so be firm. The first two phases are up for grabs and the lowest bid wins. Good luck." His chuckle fills the room. "Please, find your desks and feel free to start. Remember, you will have three days including today to work on your numbers, with your presentation to board members taking place on the third day and the subsequent awarding of the project afterward."

Heads nod in agreement around me even though I know most of us are confused about these strange and unconventional parameters for this bidding process. I haven't been out of the game that long that things have changed this much, have I?

It doesn't matter. I can roll with it. I'm used to circumstances making me adjust.

The excitement in the room is palpable as we each find our assigned desks. Eager to begin, I open my folder and shuffle through its contents: bid directives, square footage, key codes for the CAD drawings, building specifications, etcetera. These are all the things that make a girl like me happy. *Construction porn.*

With a smile wide, the adrenaline escalating, and finally feeling like I'm back in my element, it all fades when I glance up and meet the intense gaze of Ryder.

A mere five feet in front of me.

Seriously? As if tripping and falling against him wasn't enough, now I have to sit and work directly across from him.

Our eyes hold momentarily before he smiles softly and nods. Was he always this nice to me? I don't remember him being so. If he was, maybe my brain was so clouded by my constant competitiveness laced with lust for him that I never noticed it.

He shouldn't be nice to me.

Nice is distracting.

And I don't need distractions.

I need game-on.

"You ready?" I ask him, my own smile playing at the corners of my lips, a blatant and ironic attempt to distract me from my own thoughts.

"Bring it on, Denton." He flashes his own grin. "I can't wait to see what you've got."

"More than you can handle."

His laugh is quick and echoes in my head as I look down, glad to feel like we are back on a more familiar playing field. But as I start to organize the papers in the folder how I prefer them, I realize my mind is still on Ryder.

Christ, Harper. You said you weren't going to let him distract you.

Not him or his beard or his blue eyes framed by black lenses or strong jaw that pulses at the corners when he concentrates. *Nope, I'm not distracted.* Not by that or with the realization that the combination of his features is my kryptonite when it comes to a man. A little mix of the bad boy look for this professional woman. I mean just add in some tattoos and he'd be exactly my type.

But he's not. He can't be.

He's Ryder.

And I don't like Ryder. I mean, I like him and all but he's so much fun to spar with and compete against that I want that old Ryder back. The one I used to know that would bring out the best in me, make me hate him then later laugh with him. But this new Ryder is a mixed bag who I'm sure will still go head to head with me, but I like the aloofness of years ago better. The one who wouldn't glance twice at that look in my eye today or keep trying to make eye contact with me in the car after to make sure I'm okay. The guy who's not nice and doesn't catch me when I fall.

All of them are perfectly justifiable reasons why I shouldn't like him.

So why don't I believe any of them?

The bid, Harper. Start the bid.

Win the job.

Quit trying to figure everything else out first.

Chapter Six

Harper

I go through my calculations again and try to see what I'm missing. My pencil raps against the desk and when I reach for my drink, I realize it's warm and lacking carbonation. No time like the present to stretch my legs, give my eyes a short rest, and get a new drink. Maybe the respite will help my second wind to kick in.

It's only when I remove my earbuds and slip my heels on beneath my desk that I realize the war room (as we've dubbed it) is basically empty except for Alan and Ryder. Everyone else must be getting a late lunch to fortify themselves for the long night ahead.

I take a few minutes to turn all of my notes facedown on my desk and shut my laptop from prying eyes. As I stand, I take note of Alan bent over the floor model, jotting down notes about something, and Ryder leaned back in his chair, lips pursed, glasses slightly askew, and forehead furrowed in concentration while he scribbles on the paper in front of him.

Yep. He's still attractive. It's not like he's going to not be in the four hours we've been at this. I shake my head and drag my eyes away from him. Fresh air is definitely needed. Open space without him crowding it or his laugh filling it or his intelligence questioning it.

With high-caloried goodness straight from the vending machine in one hand, a cold bottle of Diet Coke in the other, I head back into the workroom with renewed vigor. I'm confident I'll be able to make some lucid sense of the equations currently a chicken-scratched mess of numbers jumbling up my pad of paper. But when I take a seat, I note that Ryder is the only one left in the room.

Figures.

Paranoia strikes the minute I look at the mess on my desk. Was that top sheet of notes askew like that? Was my pad that far forward on the desk? Did someone look at my numbers? I squint my eyes and replay my actions in my head, uncertain whether I have an overactive imagination or they've actually been touched.

"You're back?" Ryder's gravelly voice slices through the silence. His comment arouses my suspicions.

"Where's Alan?"

"He went to get something to eat. I thought you'd left too."

"Nope. I have zero plans of leaving until I'm certain I can undercut your numbers."

"Hmm."

I wait for him to say something more than his murmur and hate that it drags my mind to our past. I'd rather have his trademark sarcasm to sneak through, but that lone, drawn-out sound is all he utters. And then nothing else. His eyes are on his laptop, his attention elsewhere.

I'm just being paranoid. Next time I leave my desk, I'll need to pay closer attention to where I put things.

The room is silent except for the sounds my papers make as I shuffle them. My inherent need to start with a clean and organized desk is futile but still an effort I make.

"Missing something?"

I falter in motion, self-conscious that he's watching me. "Nope. I'm good." I refuse to look up. It's the easiest way to keep my promise to myself. The one to ignore him so I can keep focused. "Just making sure you didn't sneak a peek at my desk."

That chuckle of his echoes around the empty room as I hear

his chair creak followed by the fall of his feet on the floor. Maybe I've run him off to take his own break so now I can have some peace without the charged undercurrent that seems to be a constant when he's near.

But when his footsteps stop, they squash my hopes of him leaving right along with them.

"This whole setup is unconventional. I swear Van Dyken is trying to make us all paranoid by the time this bid is over. This whole leave-your-work-on-the-desk thing is odd. The bid's secretive, but our numbers sitting on our desk for others to snoop are free game? Makes no sense."

What's with the small talk? Ryder and I never did small talk before. We were at each other's throats one day then urged each other on the next. We did rivalry well, but never did the chatty thing or the ask-about-back-home thing. We were competitors who respected each other, but friends? No.

So his niceness feels strange to me. I don't want him to be *nice*. I just want him to quit talking so I can stop wanting to look up and see if his hair is mussed up from running his hands through it like he used to do when we'd been in the library studying until closing time. A look that used to make my insides flutter and mouth water.

"Don't you agree, Harper?"

My mind blanks when I glance up and find him right in front of me—ass resting against the front of the desk, one arm crossed over his chest while the other hand plays with the end of his beard, head angled to the side—staring at me with his eyes narrowed behind the black frames of his glasses.

That straight punch of lust I felt checking out Hot-Suit Guy hits me just as violently as it did this morning (was it only this morning?), and yet I balk at the feeling because Hot-Suit Guy is Ryder. And I can't feel lust for Ryder. I can't feel anything for him because we're competing against each other, and not for bragging rights over who's going to graduate first in our MBA program but rather for a multimillion dollar project that could make or break my career. And possibly his.

Distance between us is needed. Space. And us falling into bed where our bodies are on top of each other's like my mind keeps envisioning is definitely not space.

So I need to think about winning the bid. Then he'll be gone. The distraction over.

But as I look at him…

…his fingers…

…I'm not sure if winning in the end…

…They play with the thick end of his beard…

…is going to rid me of that crush I have on him…

Finger it. Slowly.

…or will this time with him…

Methodically.

…slowly stoke its forgotten fire back to life?

Sexily.

And I can't help but wonder if that's how he touches a woman. With that much finesse.

"Harper?"

I'll blame it on the beard. But I know it's so much more than that.

Sexual chemistry like this is impossible to ignore. Hard not to satisfy. And definitely hasn't gone away in the thirteen years since I'd seen him last. That want feels stronger, if that's even possible.

After, Harper. *Reward sex after you win. Remember?*

"Huh? What?" Pulling my gaze from his fingers, I look up to find a question in his eyes, and I'm immediately embarrassed. I swear to God he knows what I'm thinking and that in itself is mortifying.

Of course he knows. He's the one who had to bring up beard burn earlier just to make sure I knew that he'd heard me.

Seconds pass with our eyes searching each other's before he finally lets me off the hook, allows the sly smile to ghost over his lips despite the knowing look in his eyes, and then speaks. "You were answering my question."

My synapses misfire. They're stuck on my thoughts of him and his beard and wondering about his fingers and not on the here and now. And I need them to be on the here and now. "I'm sorry. I was distracted by my figures."

"Your figures?" His chuckle tells me he's not buying my lie and the amusement in his eyes sparks my need to explain how my gaze can be on him but my mind on my numbers.

"Yeah. My figures. I was contemplating if I needed to change them in case you came over here and copied them while I was gone." *There. Take that.*

But he's not offended in the least. His laugh is back and grating on my nerves as it sounds off around me. "You really think I'd steal your numbers? That that's the only way I could beat you?" This time it's him giving me a look of disbelieving shock, as if I'm crazy. But when I don't smile at him in return, his smile fades slowly. "Really? You think I'd stoop that low? I'm not that desperate," he says with a shake of his head and a quirk of a smile. "*Yet.*"

"You will be," I quip, feeling a bit more on steadier ground now that we are engaged in the bantering we are most comfortable with.

He laughs again but the sudden sincerity in his smile and softening in his eyes as he stares at me takes me by surprise. "It's been a long time, Harper."

My mind is whiplashed from the change of pace and I hate that just when I feel like I've gotten my wits about me, he says something to knock them askew again. But even with a sudden about-face in the conversation, his words cause a smile to slide onto my lips and that little flutter in my belly to come to life. "It has."

"It's good to see you again." He pauses and nods. The look on his face is unreadable. "You look good. The same but different."

"So do you."

"I'm still the same guy. You're just seeing me through different eyes."

I bite back my immediate dismissal of his words and wonder what he means by them. Have I changed that much? And if I have, how would he know it in the hours since we've reacquainted? "Perhaps." It's the only way I know how to answer.

His stare is unwavering as he gauges if my words are true. "Why the change in hair color?"

"Do you like it?" The question is out without thought and I hate that it appears I care if he likes the change.

"Yes." He nods. "But I liked you as a brunette too."

"Sometimes change is good. Sometimes it's even needed."

He studies me. "True." He draws the single word out as if he's trying to figure out what I mean so I say something quick to prevent him from drawing his own conclusions.

"Why the beard?" *Crap.* That wasn't obvious or anything. First thing off the top of my head and it's that. Lovely.

He shrugs nonchalantly, which is in direct contradiction to the knowing smile playing at the corners of his mouth. "Do you like it?"

Dear God, he's really going to ask me that after he knows damn well I do after he caught me staring?

I stutter over an answer. Can't find one other than a quick nod with a tight smile as once again he's left me rattled by being nothing but himself. Feeling this way in my early twenties was one thing, but I'm a grown woman, confident in my professional abilities and in my sexuality. I should not be rattled by anyone.

Least of all him.

But I am.

"I should get back to work." I make the excuse knowing damn well I don't want to talk about his beard anymore—or stare at it or think about it and its oh-so-good-burn—and least of all with him. "Was there something you needed?"

"Nope. *Not. A. Thing.*" His voice is slow and certain and yet he doesn't move. Doesn't look away. Just stares with questions in his eyes I can't quite read and am not sure I really want to.

"Then stop it."

"Stop what?"

"Stop staring at me. Can't you look somewhere else?"

When he smiles this time, I notice the hair around his mouth bends with its curve upward, and it takes all I have to look up to his eyes. "We sit five feet across from each other, Harp. You're in my line of sight. Besides…" He shrugs. "You're far from a hardship to look at."

My mind stumbles over his comment. It freezes. Then refires. *Did he just say what I think he said?*

"First off, *Ryd*, you're standing and not sitting, so the solution to this little problem is that you can walk anywhere else in the room and stare just as easily. There's a window over there and a whole city below. Why don't you try that? I'm sure that's more satisfying, more inspiring than looking at me. And another thing, don't call me Harp," I add for good measure before looking back down to make incoherent notes on my pad of paper, unsure why I'm mad at him all of a sudden other than the fact that he keeps flustering me and I'm not easily flustered.

And it's driving me crazy.

"Still hostile, I see."

"Still an asshole, I see," I mutter but know he can hear it.

"You're right. My apologies."

My eyes flash back to his, stare and search for the sarcasm there and see nothing but candor. The sarcasm would have been easier to deal with. "You know what? Quit being like that."

"Like what?" His face is a mask of innocence.

"Like. That."

"A little more help would be appreciated. How about an adjective or two? You know, a descriptive word?"

"*Nice.* There's an adjective for you."

"You say *nice* like it's a bad thing," he muses with a lift of one eyebrow, and the singular action only serves to infuriate me further.

"It is when it's coming from you."

"I'll remember that. I'll be sure to be an asshole from now on then. Just to you, though."

"You do that," I say with a flippant nod and my every nerve irritated and turned on by him simultaneously.

"So that's how you're going to be, huh?" He raises his eyebrows.

"Were you expecting anything different?"

Our eyes hold across the office space. They war over who's going to take the next step in this sweet rivalry of a dance we're slowly remembering the steps to.

"Never." His grin is fast and the gleam in his eyes tells me he's more than ready.

Needing to break that magnetic hold he seems to have on me, I glance toward the window—to the daylight outside. "Time to get to work," I mutter and when he doesn't respond, I glance back to him to see if he heard me. And his eyes are still on mine but his hands are starting to roll up the cuff of one of his shirtsleeves. "Better roll them up really high. It's about to get real hot for you with me back in town."

"I can take the heat just fine, Denton." His laugh is loud and pulls on my own smile to widen. "Thank you for your concern but it's not needed. I happen to be working double duty today. Superhero and badass estimator all in one."

"Oh, please." I roll my eyes as his fingers turn up his cuff. "As if."

"I'm dead serious. As a matter of fact, I happened to have the buttons of my sleeve pulled right off when I caught a damsel in distress earlier today. She debuttoned it when I saved her from a certain fall to her death."

"A fall to her death?" I laugh. Damn him for making me want to keep talking.

"It was perilous. Dirt and high heels are a treacherous combination. It says so right here in my superhero manual. There's a whole chapter on it. 'Damsels in Heels' I think is its title."

"I'm not a damsel, I don't need..." My voice fades off when my eyes flash down to where his fingers are folding back the cuff on his right arm. Because holy shit, I see ink.

A lot of colorful ink.

For the love of God, he has tattoos.

And not just a simple, one-off tattoo, but rather ink from his wrist on up to his flexing forearm and beyond where I can't see.

How did I not notice the shadow of ink beneath his dress shirt?

And when in the hell did preppy-boy Ryder Rodgers transform into *that mythical guy* who hits every single one of my buttons?

For a moment, I'm rendered incoherent. It's like I know him but know nothing about him...and now with this new discovery, he just became ten times hotter. Superficial? *Yes.* My reality? *Definitely.* And then of course I realize I was midsentence and can't even remember the comeback that was on my tongue.

Shit. That's twice in a single conversation he's done that to me.

But there were tattoos. *I'm ink-struck.* Can you blame me?

"You don't need what?" he prompts as his hands falter on his shirt cuff and bring me back to the present.

My gaze slowly lifts to meet the humor swimming in his. He's caught me looking. First at his beard and now at his tattoos. So much for being inconspicuous and acting unaffected.

I open my mouth and then close it, not sure how to respond because I sure as hell am not a damsel in distress but I'm definitely acting like the helpless heroine right now.

The door to the office sounds off and voices follow, alerting us some of the others are back from lunch.

I straighten my shoulders and stiffen my spine. "I am not a damsel," I repeat with a little less conviction than before. "I don't need to be saved, by you or anyone else."

"So I've learned." He starts to walk toward his desk and then stops and looks back at me. "A princess may not need to be saved, but she sure as shit needs to take a ride on that unicorn she's found every once in a while. He'll remind her she needs to live instead of staying locked up tight in that tower of hers."

And with that, he turns his back to me again and walks out of the room while I'm left staring after him, pretending to the others like there's nothing between Ryder and me, all the while wondering what in the hell he meant by it.

Chapter Seven

Harper

"From the information we've been given, most of us are assuming it's some type of government facility. FBI headquarters. West Coast operations hub. Definitely something to do with the government and quite possibly Homeland Security."

"Hence the need for the secrecy," my boss concludes in that resonating tone of his.

"It's only a theory." I walk toward the window of the extended-stay room in the hotel we've all been placed in and watch the people on the street below hustling to wherever they are going. It hits me how much I miss my home. Well, my home, but no longer my city.

"No, it makes complete sense. There were rumors late last year that the land had been acquired for the Department of Defense." He pauses as I pinch the bridge of my nose. "Tell me you'll win this job, Harper."

I nod my head knowing he can't me see through the line but hate that for the first time in what feels like forever, I'm not one hundred percent certain when I give him my answer. Ryder's affected me when I can't let him affect me. "That's the plan."

"You're a woman who's made some huge promises, and I'm counting on you to deliver on them."

I close my eyes for a moment and cringe at the deal I made with him. My assurance I could get him this project in turn for the job. A Hail Mary on my part to get my feet back in the water again.

"I'll deliver, Wade. No worries there."

"That's what I like to hear."

But when I hang up a few minutes later, I feel no more at ease with my promise than the first time I said it.

And it's because of Ryder. All of it.

Because I want him and can't have him. Sleeping with the enemy is not an option this time around, but the memory of his kiss way back when is enough to make me want more.

Because he looks so very different but is so much the same. A good guy who now has a bit of an edge to him, with that sexy beard and those mysterious tattoos.

Because he's irritating and knows just how to get under my skin and regardless of how hard I tell myself to shut him out, it almost seems like an open invitation to let him in.

How did Hot-Suit-Guy in the lobby and a promise of possible reward sex for getting the job turn into Hot-Suit-Guy being Ryder and oh-how-do-I-want-to-sleep-with-him but after everything in New York, sleeping with anyone who is affiliated with my work is off limits?

A deal breaker.

And now I'm tired and irritated with a long-ass day of work in front of me—across from *him* no less—because all I did was toss and turn all night. And the few times sleep did come, I dreamt of him. And not just any dreams, but ones where he was unbuttoning that shirt of his and then pulling it off.

Toned. Tanned. Etched in ink.

Of course those were my dreams—not reality—but that doesn't mean I didn't lie in bed this morning wondering if his chest is as delectable as my subconscious has created it to be.

And then there is that damn beard of his. If my dreams were any indication, it sure as hell felt like heaven between my thighs.

The problem is, now I want to know if it feels just as good in real life.

"And that's why you need to work from here for a bit," I mumble to myself as I force the thoughts from my mind right along with the memory of the incredible orgasm that ripped me from my dreams to find my fingers between my thighs earlier this morning.

There are definitely worse ways to wake up than from a powerful orgasm but the problem is now I'm obsessing over Ryder and how it would feel if my fingers were replaced by his hardened dick.

I shake my head and laugh at my lunacy. There's definitely no way I can head in to the office just yet. All it will take is one glance his way to bring my dreams to the forefront of my mind. To recall how his hands had parted my thighs before his mouth *and beard* lowered its way to taste and tempt and taunt me into oblivion. No doubt I'd be so distracted by the memory that I'd purposely make every one of my calculations equal sixty-nine or something.

Subtle. Real subtle.

God, things were much easier when the irritation factor outweighed the sexual attraction factor when it came to him. So I'll work from here for a while before I head in.

Let the dream fade. The image I made in my head dissipate. The feel of his touch lessen.

Focus on being irritated with him. That's safe. That's productive.

And time to get to it.

I look out across the square where Century Development sits opposite my hotel and then to my makeshift project plot map I've made on the wall of my hotel room. The one I started working on last night when I couldn't sleep. Color coordinated notes litter the diagram in clusters—one grouping for each building: pink for things I need to remember, blue for questions I need to ask myself, and yellow for information that links one building to the next.

I'm missing something in my calculations—I know and can feel it—but I can't quite put my finger on what it is yet. Some tiny detail that will set my numbers apart from everyone else and land me the job.

And I need to use this distraction-free space to find it.

Just as I step forward to reread my notes, the dull throb in my temples I've been ignoring all morning begins to pound stronger. My body's subtle reminder that it's been way too long since I've had a caffeine fix is demanding attention.

I'll go get coffee first.

And then I'll come back here with a clearer mind, the buzz of caffeine, and work for a bit.

Distraction free.

Chapter Eight

Harper

I never do well with spontaneity.

Case in point: I'm currently lost in this maze of a mall trying to get back from the Starbucks that took me way too long to find, and all I want to do is get to work.

Somehow I got turned around, had a mild panic attack when I came out the opposite side of the coffee house, spent way too long trying to get my bearings, and then when I finally did, couldn't find the elevator.

But I know where I'm going now. Up five floors to the sixth and then across the parking garage to my hotel. And with coffee in my system, the elevator door in front of me, and my headache subsided, my mind is already working through mental bullet points about what I can do to strengthen my proposal and trim some dollars.

Details I neglected to consider yesterday because I was distracted by a certain someone. A *someone* I am determined today to ignore.

My brain is a Ryder-free zone. Or so I told myself over and over as I waited in line for my coffee. And I repeat the mantra again as I step into the elevator car when it arrives on the second floor.

"Sixth floor, please," I ask with a polite smile to the man standing by the buttons and shift against the wall as more people pile in behind me.

Just as the door begins to close, I hear a "Hold up."

It's only two words, a common request, and yet I know who it is before his hand prevents the doors from shutting. My brain may be a Ryder-free zone, but fate has just determined it's going to be a close-quarters elevator-ride zone too.

Crap.

I grit my teeth as the doors slide back open and in those few seconds, prepare myself for seeing the man I swore I'd avoid like the plague today.

But there is absolutely nothing that could prepare me for the sight of Ryder when he walks into the car. He's shirtless, his jogging shorts are slung low on his hips, and every ink-etched detail of his sculpted torso is misted with sweat.

My subconscious was way off base. Whoever said dreams were better flat out lied. Because Ryder is mouthwateringly fine. Breathtakingly sexy.

My better sense tells me I need to look away, that I need to look down at my shoes so he doesn't see me in the car and yet I *just* can't.

My eyes refuse to obey my mind's commands.

Because everything I wondered about yesterday afternoon when he was rolling his cuffs up just came to life in full living color. The answers to the questions I had in my dreams about what his tattoos were of and their placement on his body are front and center. And the split second I have to pull myself together and glance away before he catches me gawking is lost to the pang of lust coursing through me from the combination of his testosterone-laced beauty in front of me.

Save yourself, Harper. Look. Away.

Look.

Away.

But before I can pull my gaze from the sculpted abs,

mouthwatering biceps, and intricate tattoos, they are headed straight toward me. In. Full. 3D. Living. Color.

I suck in a breath as I come face to chest with every hard inch of him. My body reacts in every visceral way imaginable. My hair stands on end as if it's trying to get closer to him, to touch him somehow. My mouth goes dry. My body tenses and aches with a delicious burn. I neglect to breathe.

Thoughts flash, hold, mesmerize. How I want to reach out, place my hands on his pecs, and feel if they are as firm as they look. How I would love to take my fingertip and trace the lines of the designs, slide it over his skin misted with sweat as his chest moves in and out from the exertion of what I assume was the workout he just finished.

The elevator jolts subtly as it starts to rise and knocks me from my lust-induced trance and back to my senses. My cheeks immediately fill with heat because it's hard to be nonchalant or downplay what I'm doing when the man I'm ogling is inches from me. But I don't look up—can't—instead I stare back down to the Starbucks cup with my misspelled name on it and hope he doesn't say a single word so I can hold tight to what dignity I have left.

Please.

The door dings. Ryder shuffles to the side to let the person beside us exit. And the minute he does, I step farther back into the car.

Get some distance from him. Create your Ryder-free zone.

The minute the thought crosses my mind though, Ryder adjusts and steps back into his position, his chest to my nose.

Seconds pass. They feel like forever. I tell myself to look anywhere else than at the tattoos or the rivulet of sweat that slides ever so slowly over his nipple. Down to my Starbucks cup again. At the ground. To anywhere. And of course I do none of the above.

Instead, I look up.

Right into the blue of his eyes.

That breath I just got back? It's lost again.

Our eyes meet, hold, lock. There is no flicker of amusement in his. The sarcastic gleam I'm used to is nonexistent. Void. And yet his eyes are filled with so much more that I'm afraid to acknowledge and at the same time dying to explore: hunger, want, need, desire.

This is the man I used to want, and yet now I understand that *the want* I knew before as a coed was nothing compared to *the desire* I can acknowledge and crave for as an adult.

The desire that can't be there. Not now. Not like this. With our history between us and the job in front of us.

And yet none of that matters as we stand like this, inches apart, as if our bodies are hovering on both sides of that fine line we know we can't cross but that our eyes are saying otherwise to.

The car dings.

More people shuffle on and off.

And yet our eyes never waver.

I think I breathe.

My hands clench the coffee cup in my hand but I don't notice the heat that burns my skin through it.

I'm afraid to move. Afraid I'll bump into him. Know that if I do, that the simple connection I was thinking of a moment ago—of his skin beneath my fingers—might be too much to bear. Desire restrained. Restraint then tested.

And so we stand in place hypnotized by the other, the elevator dings at each floor, people walk on and off, shift around us, but we remain.

His eyes flicker down to my lips. I watch as he stares at them, like how his own lips move ever so slightly before he looks back up to mine. And it's in that moment I realize the car has stopped once again, that the doors have opened, and we are the only ones left.

But I don't move. Don't make an attempt to leave the elevator on what I can only assume is my floor because my feet are rooted in place, my eyes haven't moved, and my nerves are alert with anticipation over whatever it is that might come next.

The thing I want and the thing I don't want are one and the same: a kiss.

The simple realization hits me harder than I'd like to admit. And the minute it does, I'm a flustered mess of emotions that are too strong to ignore and too ridiculous to entertain.

And then I shock back to reality. To who this is. To why I can't. To *holy shit, what am I doing?*

"I'm sorry...I uh, I've-I've—" I move in a frenzy of uncoordinated movements to try to get around him but he sidesteps and prevents me the same time his hand blocks the door from closing.

"No." It's one word but the audible restraint in his voice stops me in my tracks.

My gaze snaps back up to his. Notices the muscle in his jaw tick. Acknowledges the questions in his eyes. I part my lips to speak but don't say anything because I swear to God the air around us is so electrified that anything I say is going to set it off.

"Tell me what to do, Harper."

I'm caught off guard by my own name. The grate of his voice does funny things to my insides. And then it hits me what he just said.

Dear God. My mind fills with everything imaginable that I want him to do to me right now. With those hands of his. Those lips. That beard. And every other visible and nonvisible long, hard inch of him.

I blink and try to think of how to convert my thoughts into coherent words. I inhale unsteadily and all I do is breathe him in, and that only serves to complicate things further.

"Tell me what to do, Harper."

He repeats the words again. Uses my name in that way he has that makes it sound like he drags it over his soul on the way out, and all I can think about is that is exactly how he sounded saying it in my dream last night. Like it hurt so good it pained him.

My chest constricts as I reconcile my fiction and reality, but the problem is he's right in front of me. He's tangible—slick with sweat and oozing with every damn thing I find attractive.

He's flustered me once again.

I open my mouth.

Close it.

Open it again.

"I got off thinking about you last night."

Oh.

My.

God.

Did I just say that out loud?

The shocked expression on his face—lips parted, eyes flickering with amused surprise—is probably nothing compared to what is reflected on my face.

"I, um—I—Oh...I've..." Words escape me. Thoughts are buried in the mortification. So I run. Off the elevator. Across the catwalk. As far away from having to look at him as possible.

He calls after me but I keep going.

Have to.

Just like I did before.

Chapter Nine

Ryder

This is torture.

Pure, goddamn torture.

Even knowing so, I look up to get one more taste of said torture sitting five feet in front of me. Those damn sky-high, pink heels beneath the desk taunting me just as handily as the woman wearing them.

I groan silently at the thought, shift in my seat to calm my dick down, and refocus on the figures in front of me, but not before one more glance her way. One more taste of torment.

How can I not?

She got off last night thinking about me. And that's supposed to what? Make me not want her? Make me want her more?

What did she expect me to do after she said that to me? Just sit here five feet from her and twiddle my thumbs all day instead of wishing I was fingering her? Fucking her? Losing myself in her?

I got off thinking about you last night.

How can a sane man know this, hear those words from her mouth, and not picture the cherry red fingernails currently tapping on her keyboard sliding between the lips of her pussy, slipping inside of her then back out slick and wet, and not want to stare at her some more?

Either that or head to the bathroom and rub one out to calm the hell down.

But that wouldn't satisfy me. Hell no. Not when she's so close I can reach out and touch her. Not when I get a whiff of her perfume every time she gets up to stare at the scale model on the floor. Not when she bends over to look closer and that damn pencil skirt hugs her ass while shifting on those heels. The whole damn package has me envisioning doing so many things to her it's not even funny.

I lift my glasses and rub my eyes—something, anything—to stop me from staring one more time.

Maybe she was lying. Maybe this is her plan. Say something like that to distract me and thus throw me off my game. Cause me to think about wanting her more than fine-tuning my numbers.

And if so, it's working because my restraint only lasts so long. I look up again. It's hard not to. I take in her pink cami-whatever-it's-called with lace trim beneath that business suit of hers and think of her wearing just that.

Those heels.

And nothing else.

She glances up, our eyes holding momentarily. Enough for me to see the red flush through her cheeks before she averts her gaze and pretends like it never happened.

Nope. I'm not buying it.

She may be a ballbuster, but she's not that calculating. Not when it comes to shit like this. She may have changed, grown more confident with age, but she's still that shy girl underneath. I can see it when I talk to her. Maybe it's because I knew her before that I can see it now, but it's there. The red cheeks and flustered responses. The wide eyes and need to avoid.

Nah. It wasn't some calculated response to throw me off my game.

She meant what she said. It was a slip of the tongue that I sure as hell want to feel for myself. She fucking got off thinking about me.

And now I have to sit here the rest of the day with her right in front of me, thinking about exactly what she did to get herself off.

Either way, she wins in the end.

Because my thoughts are on her.

Chapter Ten

Harper

"You can't ignore me forever."

That voice. The one I've heard talk throughout the day. The laugh that has carried through the room at different times and felt like it was slowly removing each layer of my clothing right along with it.

This morning didn't happen.

I keep my head down and do just what he said I can't do, ignore him.

He's the enemy.

Not an irresistibly hot guy who being shirtless, sweaty, and out of breath in an elevator with me made me envision that's what he'd look like after a round of orgasm-inducing, breath-robbing, incredible sex.

He's the one standing between you and the promise you made to Wade that will let you keep your job.

And if he's going to use this strategy—the one where he renders me stupid by standing two feet from me so that I want him so bad it hurts, then I might as well play too.

Besides, nothing says game-on like a woman in heels, and I

have my favorite power-pink heels on today to prove that exact point.

Yes, I let my composure—my concentration—slip this morning. I let the sight of his skin and the bang of lust between my thighs commandeer my thoughts. Or lack thereof. But with my favorite heels and my best power suit on, I feel more in control.

No man is going to throw me off my game and make me lose this job.

That I know for sure.

Besides, it's hard to wear a pair of heels and not feel sexy.

And I need that feeling today. The sexy, the sassy, the defiant, and everything in between because I refuse to let him render me stumbling and fumbling like I did this morning.

I'm winning this bid. I can want him. I can desire him. And I can still beat him out all at the same time.

So when he asks me if I'm going to ignore him, I do just that. Keep my head down, my fingers tapping on the keyboard, and my shoulders straight.

Because this morning didn't happen.

"Harper?"

"Hmm?" I don't look up. I give him the same sound he gave me all those years ago. *He will not distract me.*

"Oh, so you can hear me. Good to know." There's humor lacing the edge of his voice and I hate that a part of me wants to look up and see if he's smiling. If his beard is curving up. "I have a sister. I'm well versed in estrogen-edged silent treatment. It works perfect for me too. You silent means you're not distracting me...so keep at it. My concentration appreciates the silence and you for it."

I don't react although every part of me bristles at the comment and the return of Ryder's trademark sarcasm.

The silence stretches. The clicking of my keyboard is the only sound in the room. I don't dare look up to see what's going on, although I have a good sense that the blackened sky in the windows at my back is a solid indicator that it's just Ryder and me remaining once again.

I continue to type. Click. Click. Hating that now that I'm aware we're the only ones left, being alone here with him is all I can think about. And dammit, my plan for not being distracted has been shot to hell.

"You're going to have to talk to me at some point," he murmurs from his desk.

"I haven't yet." I take the bait and his chuckle reinforces it.

"You just did."

"No, I merely responded so as not to be rude. Responding and *talking at some point* are two different things."

"You and your semantics." His laugh returns and pulls my eyes to him.

Damn. I shouldn't have looked because if a put-together Ryder Rodgers is hot, and a shirtless Ryder is mouthwateringly tempting, then a rumpled, tired, and hard-worked Ryder is impossibly irresistible. The one whose tie has been removed and shirt is unbuttoned enough that I can see the edges of a tattoo barely above the neckline of his undershirt.

Reminding me of just what they look like in full 3D color.

The heat returns to my cheeks again when our eyes meet, despite how hard I try to remain unaffected, but the smile he gives me is sincere and so void of the smugness I had expected.

He waits a beat before he speaks, as if he's choosing his words one by one before actually uttering them. Something I obviously need to take heed of.

"How are your numbers coming along?"

His question startles me. It's not what I expected and yet exactly what I wanted, him acting like this morning never happened.

But it did and now he's acting like it didn't.

It's like I can't make up my mind. My head wants to deny that my elevator confession ever happened while my legs want to spread apart like it did.

The one thing I do know is that the longer he stares at me, waiting for a response, the harder it is for him to deny the mocking smile from turning up the corners of his mouth in a way that fires my temper.

"I'm basically finished." He carries on as if he asked the

question to himself and is answering it. "I've made some good headway today, just paring down my presentation. How about you? You ready to take me on again? See who comes out on top this time around?"

"No. Nuh-uh. You don't—"

"*Nuh-uh?* Now I really know you're mad at me if you're breaking out the big words like nuh-uh. I take it you're struggling with your numbers then?"

I just stare at him, eyes blinking, fingers paused on my keyboard and try not to give into that placating tone of his that used to drive me bat-shit crazy.

"You don't get to do this, Ryder." I rise from my desk and walk around the front of it, needing to be on an even playing field with him.

"Do what?"

"You don't get to act like this morning never happened."

"You mean like you've been doing all day?" he asks as he crosses his arms over his chest.

"I've done no such thing." Lies. All lies.

"Really?" He laughs. With his lips and his eyes, and I know I deserve it but right now I don't want to hear or see it.

"I'm not in the mood for your games." *Can this conversation just end, please? I'm dying a slow death of indignity here.*

"But aren't you doing just that?" he asks as he cocks his head to the side and stares. "Showing up with those come-fuck-me heels on, adding a little extra sway to your hips, making sure to bend over in my perfect line of sight? I mean, you don't want me to remember what you said this morning, but you sure as fuck don't want me to forget. So tell me, Harper, if you're not playing a game, what exactly is it that you're doing? What's your end game?"

I just stare at him, slack-jawed and wanting to refute him but hating that either I'm that readable or I haven't changed as much as I thought I had from when he used to know me.

"Then again, I could have read you wrong. *But I don't think so.* Your hair may be a different color, your clothes on point, your confidence stronger, but I know how you operate."

"You don't know shit about me. Quit being—"

"I love that you're still hostile. You wouldn't be *you* without it."

And those words knock me back some—knock the fight I was instigating right out of me—because he's right and I don't have a damn leg to stand on. The tone of his voice is almost as if he admires me for it and I know that can't be, so I just stare, unsure what to say. "Fine. You want to talk? Let's talk." I fold my arms over my chest and raise my eyebrows. "And for the record, I *am not* hostile."

He chuckles. "Whatever you say, *Ice Queen*."

That nickname. The one he'd use to egg me on because he knew I hated it is like nails on a chalkboard. "You're infuriating."

"And you seem to be pissed and frustrated with me when I'm just standing over here minding my own business." He bats his eyelashes and shrugs.

"Minding your own business? Is that what you call getting in my way when I'm trying to win this bid?"

"Getting in your way?" He barks out a laugh. "That's a good one considering no one even knew you were coming, so I think you've got the story backward. You're here and now you're getting in *my* way."

I stare at him, know he's right, but refuse to give him an inch. I want to be irritated with him. For not pushing me on what happened in the elevator this morning when I don't want him to, but I also don't want that moment, that feeling, to be brushed aside. For standing here having a conversation with me like there isn't that undertone of desire simmering beneath the surface. And for being around each other after all this time and not once acknowledging that kiss we shared that night.

It's so much easier to keep those feelings at bay if I can get us back on an even playing field. To our verbal sparring. Our animosity. Our thing.

"Well, you know what they say, *ladies first*." He pushes up off the desk and takes one step toward me. "Unless, of course, you're referring to winning the bid. In that case, my chivalry is put on hold."

He stares and I'm not sure what we're doing here. It feels like we're dancing around something and yet I can't put my finger on what exactly it is.

"Chivalry is dead."

His eyes widen and then narrow. "I'm sorry you think that."

"C'mon, we work in an industry where a strong woman is considered to either be a ball-buster or a bitch. She's only successful because she's slept her way to the top or had to trade sex to be awarded a big contract." Bitterness rings in my voice. It's not directed at him, but it's still there nonetheless.

"New York."

Two words. That's all they are, spoken in that even tone of his, but they evoke such a visceral reaction in me because that means *he knows*—maybe has always known—and I hate that he does. Even worse, without ever hearing my side of the story, does he automatically think less of me because of it?

I'm momentarily derailed by the thought but know there's nothing I can do about it now other than answer truthfully. "Yeah. New York."

But when I force myself to meet his eyes again, the disappointment I expected to find in his gaze is absent. There's only kindness, only compassion, and the sight of both make me feel like I can breathe for what feels like the first time in forever.

"I found out about it earlier," he says softly.

"When you stepped out to take that call?" And I hate that I just gave away that I've been paying attention to him.

"Yes. A colleague in Manhattan found out I was bidding this project. He mentioned he thought you were bidding it too." He pauses and just stares at me. "I'm sorry. It sounds like you got the raw end of the deal."

I nod my head, draw in a deep breath, and think back to what was supposed to be a carefree night out of fun. Connecting with Jay, a friend of a mutual acquaintance, and falling into bed with him after a night of laughter and incredible chemistry. Then walking into work a week later to find the big municipality job I'd just spearheaded massive efforts to acquire *and won* was none other than

Jay's to award. The shock I felt at being blindsided. The accusations that I'd slept with him to win the job when it was nothing of the sort. Being fired for violating a strict company policy about no fraternizing or exchanging gifts—sexual or otherwise—to secure a bid. My two years in purgatory at a different job, a different position in the same industry, but on the sidelines until now. My want for a change of pace, a new environment, and my deal with Wade that if I land this Century Development project for him on a consulting basis, then I get to keep the position with his company.

A nightmare. A whirlwind. A huge lesson.

"Yeah, well…that's the breaks." I try to play it all off.

"No. It shouldn't be."

"I appreciate the sentiment but it's a fact." I shrug. "Men don't like strong women. They're intimidated by them to the point they fear them, so when a woman stands her ground, it's easier to get rid of her than rally behind her."

"I disagree."

I snort in disbelief. Not at him, but just at this conversation as a whole. I have calculations to finish, my heels are freaking killing me because he's right—I have been strutting my stuff on purpose. Now I just want this conversation to end because anything he says isn't going to change what happened, and I don't want it to end because that means the night will be over when I still want his company. And that confession to myself is hard to make but so very true.

Even though a few feet remain between us, I notice his eyes darken as he carefully mulls over his next words.

"Regardless of who *she* is—a competitor, a friend, a lover, or even all three combined—I prefer a woman who's strong. Someone I can debate with, a woman who can hold her own in an intelligent conversation, and one I can verbally spar with. I want to be met match for match. That's what I find sexy, Harper."

"I don't believe you." I reject the idea immediately, although the way he says my name—low and with inflection—causes chills to race over my skin.

When he chuckles this time, it's a low rumble that fills the empty room yet punches me squarely in the gut. His tongue darts out to lick his lips while he waits to make sure he has my attention before he continues. "I want to be challenged. In and *out* of the boardroom." His eyes lock on to mine and it takes me a minute to hear the word *boardroom* instead of *bedroom*.

But for some reason I think that's exactly what he intended.

I'm flustered by the intensity of his stare and how my mind has conveniently bent his words. "I'll challenge you all right. No worries there," I respond and know I'm speaking about both the boardroom *and* the bedroom. "But will we be friends when all is said and done? It's easy to say we will be, Ryder, but you've never walked a day in my shoes."

His gaze flickers down to my heels and there's something about his expression that tells me he's thinking of my high heels like how I think of his beard.

He takes another step forward, so now he's crossed half the distance between us.

"Those shoes look painful but sexy as hell. A double edged sword of sorts. Kind of like this whole situation with us pitted against each other is," he says in a lowered voice, despite the fact we're the only ones left in the war room. "Look, I know you're probably as thrilled about me being here as I am about you...but that's part of the dance we love, isn't it? The competition and getting the numbers right. *The battle for first.* I bet you even have a full-size body poster of me hanging on your bedroom wall to throw darts at when you get frustrated at just how good I am."

"A full size poster?" My smile is automatic.

"Yep, and I'm totally okay with it."

"*Please.*" I roll my eyes but marvel at how this man can take this conversation through so many topics and still have me smiling.

He takes another step toward me.

"This longstanding rivalry we have here is based on mutual respect. With you back in town, this will most likely be a normal thing now. Us working in close quarters and vying against each other. There will be days you're going to hate me and there are days I'm going to hate you. We will get in each other's ways. It might get a little messy, but I'm going to be nice and you're going to have to get used to that. Rest assured, I love a strong woman but have no problem going toe to toe with one. *Getting a little dirty.*" His grin is lightning quick and pulls on things deep within me it has no business tugging on. "We have a history and that counts for something with me. But at the end of the day, Harper, I have every intention of being the one who comes out on top."

It's my laugh that sounds off now and reverberates in the sexual tension slowly electrifying the air around us.

Ryder on top.

Coming on top.

Jesus. The vivid images and sudden ache those innocent words of his have just aroused within me are more welcome than not.

And wholly distracting.

Then I remember his other words—the us competing for the same bid isn't a *one-time* thing here. We're now going to be seeing each other often. The revelation evokes so many thoughts—the most prevalent one being that reward sex could be a definite, longstanding possibility here. So this time when I look back up to meet his gaze, I let the slow, suggestive smile play across my lips to taunt him.

"May the best *man* win, then."

His grin deepens, eyes sliding down my torso and back up. "Something like that," he murmurs as I push myself up to stand at full height, needing to get back to work but not taking a single step around the side of the desk.

It might get a little messy.

We stare at each other, dare each other, taunt each other as the air shifts and changes around and between us. His lips quirk up on one side. "So tell me, Harper…was I good?"

The mental whiplash is fierce but the snap of it is nowhere near as powerful as the memory of my orgasmic dream of him causes between my thighs.

The one I confessed to.

"*Hmm*," I murmur, a throwback to that debate night and a little taste of his own medicine. "I can't quite remember." My voice is coy, eyelashes batting, but my insides are on fire and welcome this sudden shift between us.

His gaze is unwavering as he shakes his head. His hands fist, forearms flex, then unfist in a visible show of restraint that's just as sexy as that muscle pulsing in his jaw. "You can't *remember*?" he asks, voice questioning as his eyes darken and intensify.

I remember everything about the dream: his touch, his murmured words, his abilities.

I know this is the point of no return. Know that my next words hold the power to either be the catalyst or the stopping point to what can possibly be between us. Since the moment I saw Ryder, I tried to hold true to my mantra—bid first, then reward sex—but I don't think I ever once believed myself.

I may be a strong woman and an ice queen in the boardroom, but there's something about Ryder Rodgers that makes me go weak in the knees.

"You know, I can't remember at all. You know how dreams are…" I let the words trail off, my playful smile and the suggestion in my tone leading him.

"Tell me what to do, Harper." Those words he said earlier are on his lips again, innocent in nature but juxtaposed to the desire clouding his eyes, are a loaded gun.

"Finish your bid. It's due tomorrow." I turn on my heel and go to round my desk, but no sooner than my first step his hand is on my upper arm, turning me back around.

Bingo.

We're face to face, bodies inches from each other, and yet mine is already set ablaze—struck by lightning—from where his hand is on my arm. Our breaths labor from the anticipation alone.

"The only thing I'm thinking about finishing right now is something I should have done a long time ago."

And without another word his lips are on mine.

And not just on mine—they take control, assault in the most pleasurable of ways, and devour any hope of being able to walk away from this job unaffected by Ryder.

There is no hesitation on my part. My reaction is reflexive.

Years of wondering and want are answered and met by the skill of his tongue as it dances against mine, the feel of his touch as his hands come up to frame the sides of my face, and the hard heat of his body as he steps into me.

It's heaven.

And hell.

It's want mixed with need.

And *I can't* warring against *more please*.

It's reawakened desire versus self-preservation.

And comparing that moment *back then* to that of *right now*.

My head spins. My body aches. It's the feel of his beard scraping against my cheek and the groan deep in his throat. It's the warmth of his tongue and the skill of his lips.

And it feels like it lasts forever, until the minute his lips break from mine and then it seems like it was only a second.

But his shaky inhalation sounds as ragged as mine when he pulls back to create distance between us.

"Thirteen years, Harper." His voice resonates with conviction. "I've waited thirteen years to finish that kiss with you. To do it again."

My lips are lax, my heart is racing, my body a combination of calm and out of control, if that's even possible. I just stare at him, eyes blinking, words not forming.

"I thought if I kissed you, got it over with, I'd get you out of my system." He shakes his head and smiles. "But I don't think it worked out quite how I wanted it to."

"Ryder." My heart is pounding, voice breathless.

"Tell me what to do, Harper."

Chapter Eleven

Ryder

"What do you want, Harper?"

She looks at me—eyes wide, lips parted—and every part of me begs to dive back in and take another taste. To back her up against that desk behind her and finish this striptease of temptation we've danced in the past forty-something hours.

But I wait for an answer.

Need one.

And it's killing me to turn my back on her and head toward the door instead of stepping back into her, but I'm not doing this again. Not going to let her run away from me because she's too scared to admit what she wants.

"Wait! Where are you going?" The panic in her voice hits my ears, boosts my ego, and only makes it that much harder not to break stride.

It's time to force her hand.

"You didn't answer the question," I toss over my shoulder.

"Ryder?" Desperation causes her voice to break.

I dislodge the first of the double doors from the wall and close it. "You have a history of running from me." I secure the bolt so it can't be opened from the outside. Not that it matters though because the last person left this office over two hours ago. We're alone.

Completely alone.

"It's not a hard decision. I'm not asking you for forever. I'm just asking you for tonight. For right now. To figure out what this is…and I'm not going to let you run away this time. Not until I hear you give me an answer." Turning my back to her once more, I dislodge the second door and am in the process of securing it when she finally speaks.

"*You.*"

My hands falter, heart does too, before I step back and meet her eyes. She's come half the distance and is standing there in those pink heels, with her hair falling out of her ponytail from where I held it when we kissed, and all I can think about is how I want to pull that hair tie out and watch it come undone as I make her come undone.

"What was that?" I ask, wanting her to be sure of her decision because once she says yes, there is no damn point of return for me.

"You, Ryder. The answer to your question, *what do I want*, is I want *you*."

Thank fuck.

We stare at each other for a beat, my dick telling me to hurry the hell up, use the desk, the chair, anything to ease this need she's created inside of me. But my head is telling me to think this through. To be smart. To not put her in a position like the prick in New York did in any way, shape, or form.

"You sure?"

She gets this coy smile on her lips that makes my balls tighten in anticipation over whatever is to come next.

"Yes."

The Ice Queen melts.

Chapter Twelve

Harper

I'm about to have reward sex.

The thought flickers and fades through my mind as Ryder crossed the distance between us with a slow, purposeful walk. His shoulders square, his eyes intense, his smile suggestive, and everything about him screams he's about to take what he wants, no holds barred.

Thank God.

I don't give a second thought to the fact that I haven't won the bid to get the reward.

I don't think twice to ask him to check that the door is locked.

I don't question a single thing because thinking's impossible right now.

"Harper." It's a question. A plea. A command.

And just like that I step into him. Into his arms and his hands and the steeled length of his body as our lips meet. The kiss isn't gentle by any means. It's packed with need and greed and is a manifestation of the pent up desire we've held at bay over the last two days and for the last thirteen years.

His hands are everywhere on me yet I still can't get enough of them. And of him. His taste is a torment all its own. The way he teases with his tongue against mine is slow and seductive, driving me mad, and when I'm about to be drugged under by the subtle bliss of it, he changes tactics. He demands more from me. With his hands and his lips and his words and that little groan in the back of his throat that sounds exactly like how I feel—overwhelmed with need and dazed by this newfound, different type of desire I've never experienced before.

We're slow and steady with a tinge of desperation. Our kisses, our encouragement, our movements. It feels like it lasts forever and doesn't last long enough.

And then my hips hit the desk behind me, and it's like a switch has been flipped, our bodies ready to sate and take and claim. We're a desperate rush of movements. His hands pushing my blazer off my shoulders. My fingers working the buttons on his shirt. His slipping the cool silk of my camisole over my head. My hands on his belt and unzipping his pants. His fingers unzipping my skirt.

All the while our lips meet, then separate.

Hurry.

A lick of his tongue against mine.

God, I want you.

I nip his bottom lip with my teeth.

You're gorgeous.

His lips on my neck, at that spot right below my ear.

I want to touch you everywhere at once and want to savor you at the same time.

His mouth on my nipple through the lace of my bra. The heat, the wetness, the pressure of him sucking, but muted from the fabric so it leaves me wanting more.

We can savor later. Just touch me. Everywhere. Now.

My fingers finding their way beneath his waistband to wrap around his cock. Our mutual groans when I begin to work up and down its long, hard length.

Christ, Harper. Fucking Christ that feels good.

The feel of his beard over my breast as his mouth finds his way back up my body, all the while shoving his pants down his hips to grant me better access to stroke him.

His mouth is on mine again with a fervent ardor. Gone are the sips and tastes. Now it's heat and passion and urgency and demand. And then his fingers find their way between my thighs. I swear I try to remember to kiss him, but I can't render a thought let alone make my lips move because I'm on sensation overload. His fingers part me, dip into me, and tease me before sliding back out, coated in arousal, and make their way to my clit. No, there is not kissing him back. There is only wanting to spread my thighs wider to enable him to touch me more.

And so I do just that, sit my butt down on the desk behind me and part my thighs. Ryder stays where he is and outstretches his arm, fingers still in me, and meets my eyes. They're clouded with lust but it's the half-cocked smile on his lips, carnal and rapacious, that holds me rapt as his gaze scrapes ever so slowly down my body to where his fingers are buried deep within me.

His eyes remain there, pulling my own down with it, so that we're both watching his fingers work in and out of me. It's erotic. It's intoxicating. It's damn near incredible.

I burn and I ache and I tense up but want to melt into a pool of bliss. There are so many damn sensations that I'm not sure which one to focus on: the friction he adds to my clit, the pressured slide down my seam before he plunges his fingers into me, or his expert manipulation of my nerves inside.

He watches his hands pleasure me and I watch him. His eyes are intense, concentration etched on his face, dick swelling as his hand works over and over and over in sync with his fingers within me.

Over the edge I fall. The lightning strike of ecstasy hits me with forewarning but there's no way I can prepare for it. It burns hot and bright and the current reverberates out to my limbs and then back to my center again as my muscles pulse around his fingers.

I think I cry his name. I'm not sure because there's a buzz in my ears almost as strong as the pounding of my pulse so I wouldn't be able hear it even if I did. When I open my eyes, he wears a haughty smirk that says *I told you it would be good.*

And just like every other part of our tumultuous relationship back then and right now, that arrogance pulls on me, challenges me, makes me want to push his limits.

In seconds, I'm off the desk and on my knees with his cock, thick and heavy, in my mouth. His gasped growl fills the room around us as his hands find the back of my head and grip my hair.

I use my tongue and hands and lips to tease and taunt and torment him. A lick of my tongue. A suck of my lips. A twisted stroke of my hand around his shaft. A slide all the way down onto it until its thick head hits the back of my throat. His groan in the air and his fingers tensing on my scalp before I start all over again.

I work him in and out of my mouth with lips pulled tight to add that extra suction. His ass flexes beneath my palm as he thrusts himself farther into my mouth. My own body reacts to the taste of him, the feel of him, and the power of knowing I can pleasure him.

That sweet ache is back in me and starting to burn bright again. My hunger for him is ravenous, so I work his cock harder, wanting that moment where he loses control to be in my hands, by my mouth, and at the same time needing him inside me desperately. Filling me. Pushing me. Breaking me down to a whimper until I cry out his name in pleasure.

My mind wars whether to let go or to hold on while his pre-cum hits my taste buds and his dick begins to swell. He's so large, so engorged, and I'm so turned on I have to concentrate on drawing in air.

I did this to him. God what a heady, arousing feeling.

Just when I decide to go for it, suck him off and swallow every last drop he has to offer, he pulls his dick from between my lips with a popping sound. I don't even have time to protest or react because he hauls me up and pushes me over the edge of the desk. Before I have time to say a word, I hear the telltale rip of foil and within moments his hands are firmly on the sides of my ass, and his dick pulsing at my wet and ready entrance.

"Do you actually think I'm going to let you suck me dry? You don't get to control this, Harper." He pushes in about an inch, my body burning in the most desirable of ways—from stretching to accommodate his girth and from the havoc the ridge on his head is causing on every single one of my nerves. I clench around him, beg for more. "I do."

And with those last words he slams into me from behind so that I can feel the wake of my nerves being willingly assaulted in every inch of my body. My moan sounds out in the room, hits my ears, and yet all I can do is feel as he bottoms out in me and grinds his hips so every part of me is filled to the hilt with him.

Good God that feels incredible. But nothing like when he starts to move in and out of me. Slow at first. Then a bit more demanding. A lot more pleasurable.

His hands are on my hips, his fingers bruising my skin. My arms are laid out across the desk, over plans and pencils and notebooks, and I don't care. Each time he thrusts back into me, the bite of the edge of the desk brings me back from the brink of an orgasm.

Our sounds fill the rooms. The slap of skin together. His harsh pants. My soft pleas for more. His guttural groan as he demands that I tell him what I want.

Harder.

Faster.

Deeper.

Don't stop.

It's the slow burn tinged with the edge of a wildfire. The gentle swell of sensations overtaken by the huge surge of unfettered desire. The eye just before the storm hits.

And when it hits, it's everything all at once. It's touch and taste and scent and sound. It's *don't move* and *don't stop*. It's white-hot heat flashing beneath my closed eyelids and sweltering embers igniting into flame. It's me being so consumed in the orgasmic haze that it's not until my name is a broken groan that I realize he's coming too.

My body writhes on the desk as his hands hold tight onto me. Each buck of my hips causes a growl from his throat and a tensing of his fingers into my flesh. He leans over and wraps his arms around me and hugs me from behind.

It's an unexpected move that causes so many thoughts and fears and worries that have no place in the moment to scatter back into hiding as he lies like this on top of me, bent over the desk. Our hearts calm some, our breathing eases, and the warmth of his lips and coarseness of his beard are a comforting feeling against my back.

"I guess we have to move," he murmurs after a bit followed by a chuckle.

And it's not like I didn't know we were in the office. On Alan's desk. In the same place we're to submit proposals in the morning that quite possibly could derail whatever this is between us here, but with my body satisfied, my brain begins to realize this.

"It's a little late to worry about it now," I murmur as he stands up and pulls out of me—both his warmth and the feeling of fullness gone at the same time.

"True," he says at my back. "But considering I plan on doing that again within the hour, I think it might be best if we move it to a bed. Or a kitchen table. Or wherever the hell you want to have it so long as it's not the office."

I'm up off the desk in an instant, the dark promise of his words reinvigorating me as his low chuckle at my reaction resonates in the room around us.

Our eyes lock. Our smiles widen. And we stand there, spent, exhilarated, and enamored. Him in his dress shirt unbuttoned and undershirt pushed up to his armpits granting me only a partial view of those tattoos I want to lick. And me in my bra and heels and one leg in my skirt. We're a picture of urgency and desperation. Of holding a torch for someone for years and finally getting the chance to light it and see if it works in the dark long enough to find your way to each other. Of desire recognized, attraction undisputed, and the need for more paramount.

The flash bang of lust between us has been taken care of.

Now I want to take my time with him.

Trace my fingers over his tattoos. Suck on his nipples. Feel his hips beneath me thrusting as I lower myself slowly, inch by inch down onto his cock.

"I guess we should get dressed to get undressed again, huh?"

"Hmm."

It's that sound from our past again. The one that lit the fire so long ago. The only difference though is when I hear it this time, I know what he means by it.

And this time I laugh.

Chapter Thirteen

Ryder

Her throaty moan fills the room. She's still asleep but I slide my tongue up and down the pink of her pussy anyway. I tease the inside of her thighs with the coarse end of my beard. I blow on her clit, flick my tongue over it again and again before sucking on the little nub, earning me another sound.

"Mmmm. Feels so good." Her murmur is groggy, and I know she thinks she's dreaming this, but I really am licking her pussy and about to make her come.

Because we may have done a lot of things last night when we finally got back to her room—till all hours of the morning type of things—but the one thing I didn't do was give her a good and proper beard burn. We were so lost in the moment, so damn desperate to have more of each other, that there were a lot of things we missed that I plan on making up for…but this was a priority.

Besides, what man doesn't like to eat a little pussy for breakfast?

So I start the process all over again, but this time with a little more intention. The first one was an I'm-going-to-make-you-think-it's-a-dream and this one is going to be the I'm-going-to-wake-you-up.

A part of me is hoping she doesn't wake right up. Her scent, her taste, are so goddamn addicting that I don't want to leave this bed. Or rather, I don't want to leave my spot between her thighs.

So I lick again. I use my hands to gently push her thighs father apart, take my beard and tease her sensitive skin with it, and then begin fingering her with smooth, slow strokes to match my tongue's rhythm on her clit.

She murmurs my name. One of her hands comes down to fist in my hair and push my face harder into her. So this time I dart my tongue inside of her, lick it around, and suck on the opening to her pussy.

I know the moment she fully wakes up. There's a gasp in the room, a tensing of her thigh muscles and a tighter grasp on my hair as she tries to sit up. "Ryd—what—oh, God that feels good." Her words fade to moans as she lifts her hips up into my face. My tongue and fingers work her to the brink, all the while making sure to let my beard leave its mark on her. That sting of coarse to smooth, of tough to soft, of me to her.

"That feels like heaven," she says in that sexy rasp of a morning voice that hardens my dick as I think about how she took me in her mouth last night without a moment's hesitation. How I know she was determined to suck me off and drink me dry, and so now I'm here to return the favor.

"What time is it?" she murmurs as I add an extra finger to the mix so I can stretch and fill and assault her nerves even better.

My fingers still, my tongue slips out of her, and I lift my eyes to meet hers over the mound of her pussy.

"Excuse me? Am I doing this so poorly you're thinking about work?" I ask, half joking, half serious, and one hundred percent knowing she's trying to control the situation.

I let her think she was in charge last night. I let her set the pace, let her say she wanted me, let her suck my cock like she was thirsty for more, and yet right now, this is me taking back that control.

"No. I didn't mean—I—"

"Relax," I chuckle with my lips to her flesh, still swollen from last night. She tenses and then her sigh becomes a moan. Her legs fall open wider and right into my plan of attack.

I lick again. In her. Around her. Up and down.

"We have the bid…ohhhhhh."

I run my beard up and down her seam each time before dipping my tongue into her again.

"It's due in a few hours…oh God, yes."

I start the process again.

"But…"

Her taste changes. Becomes muskier. Tells me she's falling just into that comatose realm where pleasure swamps reality. Her fingers grip the sheets beside her hips. Her breathing becomes labored.

And then I stop: my hands, my tongue, my beard.

"Don't stop!" Her head snaps up as I look at her from my perch between her thighs.

Now I've got her attention.

I kiss her ever so gently on her clit before sliding my beard over it as I watch her eyes widen and darken with desire. Her hair is a mess. Her lips are unpainted. She has creases from her pillow on her cheek. I'm between her thighs and her taste is on my tongue.

She's never looked more beautiful.

"Stop talking, Harper. Stop thinking. Last night I let you take the lead. I know how much you need to feel in control and so I let you set the pace. Now it's my turn. Now it's my mouth on your pussy. My beard on your thighs. Work does not enter our bedroom. Figures do not matter. The only ass that's going to happen to get beat in here is my hand smacking your beautiful one while I ride you from behind." I dip down, take another lick of her addictive taste before I lift my face back up, no doubt with her juices on my beard. "This is you. This is me. And nothing else. So lie back. Relax. And let me enjoy the taste of your pussy. I dare you not to come."

And with that—with her eyes wide and lips in the perfect shape of an *O*, I dive back in, challenge issued, and begin to work my magic while I watch her eyes slowly roll back into her head.

Chapter Fourteen

Harper

"Where's your dartboard?"

His voice pulls on me to look but I'm so sexily satisfied that it's hard for me to think of anything else than that tingling burn on my inner thighs, my abdomen, and my neck that is a subtle reminder of where Ryder's been, what he's done, and that he intends on coming back for more so I don't forget.

Beard burn *is* a real thing.

And *oh my God* is it everything I wanted it to be and then some.

I turn my head to look over at him through the dawn-filled sky-lit room, where his face is snuggled in the pillow inches from mine, one eye hidden, the other looking as sleep-and-sex drugged as I seem, and the world feels right.

"My what?"

"Your full-size-poster dartboard of me that you use to get your aggression out."

My laugh is soft. "I forgot to pack that one when I moved out here."

"So you're really here to stay?" There's what sounds like hope in his voice and it does funny things to my insides, similar to what his tongue did to me earlier this morning.

"That's my plan. Win the bid. Have reward sex. Find a place to live. You know, the usual."

His laughter rumbles the sheets. "Have reward sex?"

"Yep." And so I fill him in on my plan that first morning a couple days ago. It feels like yesterday and forever all at the same time.

"Reward sex. Huh. Then what was last night?"

"Reward sex," I state with a definitive nod as I reach out and trace the lines of his tattoos that my tongue came close and intimate with last night. My body breaks out in chills at just the thought of it. "I think maybe I had my eye on the wrong prize."

"So you finally got it right?"

"Yep. It took me thirteen years. A reward was definitely needed."

He laughs again but this time the sheet slips off my bare breasts with its vibration, and I have a feeling that part was on purpose. His eyes slide down, stare at my pebbled nipples from the air of the room and the sudden want to have him again, before looking back up to mine with a mixture of desire and honesty.

"I never figured you for the blonde bombshell, Denton." His words boost my ego in a way that's unexpected. Like this was all supposed to happen this way. Like he appreciates me more now because he knew where I came from.

"And I never figured preppy boy Rodgers to be the tatted, bearded hottie from the security line that pushed every single erogenous button on my body."

"Every one?" he asks with a lift of his eyebrows.

"Yep."

"Hmm. I think there are a few we can find yet."

"Is that a challenge?" I ask coyly.

"Isn't that how we work together best?" All I can do is sigh at his words and nod my head. Look at my hand on his chest and smile at the truth in his words. "I looked for you the next day, you know."

"What?" My voice remains even while my head shrieks the

word. *Is he saying what I think he's saying?*

"Yeah. It was like I'd always looked at you from afar—the girl hiding behind her shyness—and thought you were pretty."

"Oh, please. Me? I was a mess. I didn't do my hair. I wore those yoga pants and hid my boobs behind that baggy sweatshirt."

"Now that? That was a travesty," he murmurs, smile lighting up his face as he reaches out and cups my breast and just leaves his hand there with his thumb rubbing back and forth over its sensitized tip.

I close my eyes and absorb the sensation and when I open them back up, his eyes are locked on mine, intense and unrelenting.

"I went to your place the next day after asking around to find out where you lived but you'd left already. You were already moving on to your new life in New York and I was about to start mine...so I let it go."

"Why'd you try to find me?" I ask the question I'm not sure of the answer to, the confident woman I am now wanting to know, the shy girl I used to be needing to know.

"There was always something about you, Harper. Sure you were horribly shy and in a constant state of fluster, but there was something about it that was intriguing. You were pretty but didn't know it. And hell, when you went head to head with me in class, you were a different person. You were confident and demanding and I respected that. I hated you for it...maybe even resented you for it...but I damn well respected you for it. Even when you beat me time and again."

My grin is quick but my hand is quicker as I reach beneath the sheet and grab his dick in my hand. It's already thick and heavy against his abdomen and makes my own body surge to life. His gasp when I stroke my hand over it is all I need to hear to know that he feels like I do right now. "I'll beat you again, too," I murmur. "But this time, it will be with my own two hands." I shift from my position, pulling the sheet off us as I do, and his laugh rings out in the room.

"The lady has mad skills in the joke department."

"I've got mad skills, all right." I lick my lips as I look down at him in all his glory. At his impressive cock, up and over his incredible chiseled abs, to the start of his tattoos on his right ribcage that go up in a dizzying array of lines and graphics, to where his beard rests on the top part of his chest. Damn. I meet the amusement in his eyes again as I shift over his thighs and rest my ass there. "I intend to show you just how mad they are right now."

I dip my head down and lick my tongue over the head of his cock. His sharp inhale of breath is audible, and when I look up I see he's arched his head back, his hands fisted in the sheets, and all I can think of is how is it possible that I want more of him already?

Right up until I see the flashing light of the clock on the nightstand to the left of his pillow.

"Oh my God!" I cry out, causing him to snap his head up as I scramble off of him in a frenzied panic.

"What? What is it?"

I'm already off the bed, my mind a cluster of thoughts, and I can't pinpoint which one I want to tackle first.

"It's six-thirty. I need to finish the details on my proposal." I hit the far end of the wall and head back the other way to get my robe. "What if we missed something last night when we left? What if you dropped the condom wrapper and didn't see it? I'm the only woman in that room and so— What if we didn't put the stuff on Alan's desk back right and he questions it? What if—"

Ryder's hands catch my shoulders and pull me against him, my back to his front. "Calm down," he murmurs against my shoulder, beard tickling and dick tempting me from where it's pressed against my backside. "Calm down."

"Ryder, I—"

"You have plenty of time. You said yourself you were done last night. You just needed to tweak a few things. Right?" I nod my head despite the worry still rifling through me. "Damn, and I thought I'd sex you up so good you'd forget your numbers."

"Funny. Don't you know that while sex makes men fall asleep, it reinvigorates women? Makes them sharper. So thanks for making me razor-edge sharp this morning."

He starts to say something, stops himself, and then barks out a laugh. "Fucking great."

I shrug and swat his hands off my waist. No more touching or else I'm going to do what I really want to do—turn around and finish what we were just starting. "Shoo. Go so I can get ready."

"Nothing like being shown the door while your dick is still hard." That laugh again. This time it's followed by a slow and steady scrape of his beard up the line of my shoulder, leading to an open-mouthed kiss at the base of my neck. "Take your time. I'll head back to my room, get dressed, and head in. I'll make sure everything is kosher there while you take a shower and finish your proposal here. Everything is fine, Harper. The bid will be fine. We will be fine regardless of the outcome. And we'll figure things out from there because this. Here"—he motions a hand to the bed and then back to me—"will be happening again."

"Well, one of us is bound to get reward sex tonight," I chuckle.

"May the best man win." He presses a kiss to my shoulder that makes my stomach flip-flop from the butterfly wings starting to flutter.

"May the best woman win. It's sexist to assume it's going to be a man." My smile is automatic. Winning would be the absolute icing on this cake. Let's see if he takes the bait.

"Semantics." I feel his mouth spread into a smile against my shoulder. "But okay. I guess we can say, may the best *wo*man win." There's a pause. I can all but hear his mental gears click into place. "*Wait*. That's bullshit. There's only one woman bidding."

"Exactly."

Chapter Fifteen

Ryder

"You're looking damn chipper this morning," the security guard in the line says with a smile when I pass him by.

"Because it's a damn good morning," I say. *And night. And hopefully day.* "Have a good one."

The elevator is empty, my arrival to the office quick; all the while Harper's on my mind. Everything about her. Every minute of last night. Each sound she made. Each smile she gave me. Every ounce of hunger that remains to have her again.

How stupid was I to tell her this was just about last night. One night. There's so much more there, it's blaringly obvious. But first we need to see how today goes.

Then reward sex.

Gotta love a woman who rewards herself with sex. *That's so damn hot.*

When I push open the door to the war room, I'm surprised to find Patrick here already.

"Christ, Rodgers," Patrick all but yelps, causing us both to jump, equally startled by each other. I hiss as my coffee sloshes over and scalds the skin of my hand, and when I look back over to him, Patrick is on his knees, picking up the papers he knocked to the ground off of Harper's desk.

I should help him since I'm the one who startled him, but I'm more concerned with what Harper and I did or didn't leave here last night.

"I thought this place would be dead," I say, eyes homed in on seeing if Alan's desk remains as unscathed by our sex as I remember it being.

Whew. We're in the clear.

No condom wrapper in sight. Papers are stacked neatly.

Let's hope there are no grip marks from her hands...or boob marks, from where she held on.

"You scared the shit out of me," he says with an audible exhale as he puts the last of the fallen papers back on to Harper's desk before focusing his attention on the floor model in front of him.

I can't help but laugh seeing Mr. Smooth and Asshole look so damn startled. "Yeah, well, I wanted to get a jump on finalizing a few things. You?"

Shit. *Her panties.* Those are her panties.

On the floor.

Just beneath the leg of the desk.

How did we forget those?

"Same here," he says, preoccupied with the model, allowing me to stoop down, casual as can be to pick up and then stuff a very pink, sexy-hot scrap of lace into my pocket. "This was a brutal one, wasn't it?"

I stare at him, relieved he doesn't give me a second look before he bends back over to take notes on the trickiest building in the bid package and wonder if that hung him up like it did me. "Definitely. There's so much security and electronics in that building it's hard to not feel like your numbers are high when you think they are as low as you can go."

"Exactly. Perfectly said." He nods, crosses his arms over his chest, looks back to the model, and then back up to me. "It's going to be a close one, I think."

"Always is." I sit down at my desk and start up my laptop. "Good luck." *You're going to need it.*

"You too. You too."

Chapter Sixteen

Harper

"How'd it go?" Ryder murmurs from behind me as I bite back the yelp from not knowing he was there.

"Good. Great." I nod my head, the adrenaline rush ten times stronger than I've felt in forever, and it feels incredible.

To be back in the game.

To be confident in my numbers.

To know reward sex is a definite.

And to know said reward sex is with Ryder.

"You? How do you think your presentation went?" I ask, my hands still trembling and the look on the board's faces still etched in my mind. I've got a few hours to kill so I'm sure I'll overthink what exactly those expressions meant a couple of thousand times while we wait.

"It went well," he says with a nod and a tone to his voice that sounds exactly like I feel: negatively optimistic and positively pessimistic.

"Good. I'm glad." We walk a few more steps back to the war

room where lunch is being catered, the last meal before they decide our fate, and wonder how we will handle whatever happens next.

And if I get to keep my job.

Or lose it.

At least I have last night to relive over and over while I sit and wait.

Those memories will definitely pass the time.

No complaints here.

Chapter Seventeen

Ryder

"Good luck."

I look over to Harper sitting at her desk where this whole thing between us unknowingly began and nod my head with a smile. "See you on the flip side," I say as Mason Van Dyken's assistant waits at the door to usher me back into the conference room.

I try to play it cool, like being called back in a second time is a normal thing in this situation, but it's not. The furrowing of Harper's brow when they called my name says she thought the same thing.

We'd been waiting for them to reconvene all of us and announce the award of the bid, so this feels off to me.

"Gentlemen," I greet them as I walk into the room.

"Please take a seat," Mason asks as he gestures to the chair in front of the four men. I do as I'm told and wait for them to speak.

Silence stretches as they shuffle documents in front of them—trying to look official—before looking back up so that all four sets of eyes home in on me.

"I'd like to start by thanking you for accepting our invitation to the bid."

The death words. The "thank you but you're about to get denied the job" type of death words.

My hopes fall. My pride and ego take a kamikaze spiral down with them.

"Thank you for inviting me."

"This project is rather unique. It's highly sensitive and extremely private, as you've inferred by this whole process. Having you bid on a job when you can only guess about its nature must be difficult. And we understand that more than anyone. You've probably guessed it's a government facility due to the secrecy, and if that were the case, then you'd be right."

Why are they telling me this if I didn't get the job?

"We here at Century Development would like to offer R Squared Management the first two phases of the project formally called DOD Project 427."

I stare at him, try to feign like I'm playing it cool while I'm silently slack-jawed, wide-eyed, and shocked as shit that I finally beat out Harper Denton.

Holy fucking shit.

Play it calm, Ryd. You knew you had this.

"Thank you so much, sir. I promise we'll live up to the standards you expect and get the job in under budget and on schedule." He repeats the last words with me and chuckles at the mantra.

"You look a little surprised, son."

I look over to meet Mason's questioning stare. "Not to undercut my abilities, sir, but to be honest, I expected Meteor to be the lowest bidder." *Did I really just say that?*

"Tom Grant, here. Nice to meet you, Ryder," the gentleman to the right of Mason says.

"Nice to meet you too, sir." My eyes narrow as I try to figure out why all of a sudden Mason is whispering something into his ear, a little conference before a few nods are had. Something's off here.

"This bid was to be handled with the utmost integrity."

"As they all are," I reply with a nod, trying to feel out the sudden change of vibe in the room.

"There were color-coded folders handed out at the beginning of the project. Each folder was unique in that it held a different set of numbers for each participant to bid from."

I lower my head for a moment, shake it with my eyes closed as I try to process what he just explained. "So what you're saying is we were all bidding the concept of the project but all had different numbers?" *Who the hell does that?* A part of me feels played while the other part is extremely intrigued as to the reasoning behind it.

"Exactly. The bid numbers were the same for all of the buildings except for one. That building's square footage was different for each of you. We tracked those individual numbers with the color-coded folders."

"And you are with what company?" I know I may be out of line asking but I deserve to know.

"I work for a specific branch of the Department of Defense whose interest lies in the project. I'm here to oversee the bid process and the overall project to make sure we have the right people for the job. People we can trust. People with integrity. People who we can leave unsupervised with this huge project and not worry that aspects of it will fall in the wrong hands."

I stare at him, try to read the etched lines in his face and what he's saying behind his words. This is all so cloak and dagger-ish, and I wonder what I'm missing here. My first thought is it's a training facility for the FBI or some other security agency. Pieces start to click—the different set of buildings: dorm-like rooms in one, a medical-type facility in another, classrooms in yet another area, the mandatory fence and clearance area away from the actual buildings. While the need-to-know aspect is odd to me, it is slowly starting to make sense.

"Okay...I hear what you are saying...but *why* have us bid differently if we're going to have to reconfigure our numbers in the end?" I think of the request to leave folders on the desks. The directive that all bid items were to remain in the war room. Things start to line up and yet still seem so unconventional.

"Because this project is important. We need to know the person awarded the contract can keep things confidential. That they won't allow the information to fall in the hands of people who might want to use it for the wrong reasons. I'm saying too much… You'll get all your answers once the ink of your signature is dry on the contract."

"Okay." *What are you not telling me?*

"What he's trying to get to," Mason interrupts, "is you weren't the lowest bidder, Ryder."

If he didn't have my attention before, he definitely has it now. "I don't understand."

"There were two bids that came in lower than yours. Actually there were two identical bids, to be honest."

"But that's not possible." If there are two sets of numbers, there can't be matching bids.

"*Exactly*." He nods for emphasis. "And hence we have thrown those two bids out. They either co-conspired, worked together, or someone cheated and stole the numbers."

"So you throw both out? If someone cheated, that doesn't seem fair."

"Are you trying to talk yourself out of getting this job?" Mason chuckles but his eyes flash a warning that I heed with caution.

"No. That's not the case. I'm thrilled to have been awarded the job but I'm just trying to understand. Who had the low bids?" I want to know and don't want to know, and Mason's expression reflects the same confusion I feel.

"Meteor and Lux."

Fuck.

Fuck. Fuck. Fuck.

Patrick. This morning. The papers that fell by Harper's desk. Was he looking at them? Were they in his hand when I first walked in or did he really knock them off the desk when I startled him.

Think, Ryder.

Fucking think.

"And so you disqualified both of them." It's not a question, merely a statement, and yet I know they feel like I am questioning them anyway.

You walked in the room.

Tom clears his throat and looks to his left, where another person sits and then looks back to Mason before meeting my eyes again.

"Given the peculiar set of circumstances one of the bidders left her job under, we're under the mindset that it's best that we throw both sets of numbers out."

Left *her* job under. I think of Harper's comment this morning. May the best woman win. And know they are referring to Harper—can't be referring to anyone else since she's the only female bidding—and reject the idea that she cheated immediately.

And yet they won't give her the bid because of New York. Her words echo in my head: *When a woman stands her ground, it's easier to get rid of her than rally behind her.*

I feel sick to my stomach.

Did Patrick already have the papers in his hand when I walked in? Or did he accidentally knock them off Harper's desk when I startled him?

I try to remember. Will myself to see it all again.

They were in his hand.

Are you sure though? Accusing someone of cheating is a huge deal.

Goddamn right I'm sure. Harper wouldn't risk this chance by cheating. Besides, she wouldn't need to.

"I was in here early this morning. I startled Patrick when I walked in. We both jumped and I burned my hand spilling my coffee. When I looked up, he was putting papers onto Harper's desk. At the time, I thought maybe he'd knocked some of Harper's papers onto the ground because I'd startled him...but now that I think back, I'm pretty damn sure he had them in his hand before he dropped them."

"Are you accusing him of cheating?" Mason's back gets straighter and he sits up taller.

"I'm just telling you what I saw. It was just the two of us this morning before anyone else got here. Harper's meticulous, Mason. She wouldn't leave loose papers on her desk. They'd be in the color folder, not sitting there so anyone could just look at them."

What in the hell are you doing, Ryder? This job is huge. HUGE. So why are you risking it?

Because integrity matters. Winning the fight when the others have their hand tied behind their back is not right. *It's dirty.*

And getting dirty with Harper is one thing.

Being dirty this way is completely different.

"So what is it that you are suggesting, Mr. Rodgers?"

A woman is not worth giving this job up for. Don't be stupid. Don't do it.

"I may regret this in the end, but let me review their numbers." The looks on their faces tell me what I'm saying is as crazy as what I feel like I'm saying. "It has to be the one building that's off, right? So let me figure out what that number should be with the original bid set package. I'll most likely get close enough to their numbers and then you'll have your answer over who cheated."

"And what if you aren't the low bidder anymore?"

My heart is pounding in my chest and my knee is jogging up and down. I purse my lips and look each one of them in the eye before answering. "Then I trust you to award the bid to the person you feel is most deserving in skill, experience, and ethics."

Fuck, I just screwed myself, didn't I?

"Why would you even offer this?" Tom asks.

"I don't know," I say as I shove up out of my chair and pace the room, hand on my neck and disbelief in my brain. "Maybe because I want to win the bid fair and square. I won't accuse Patrick of cheating unless I know he did and I don't think it's fair to assume it's Harper because of something we don't know all the details of. I'd think it would be the opposite. If you're trying to get your reputation cleared, you'd give a great bid and do it free and clear...but that's just me."

Easy, Ryder. One night of hot sex does not mean you side automatically with her. Your dick doesn't make the decisions here. You do.

And yet I still know she wouldn't cheat. Why would she have to? She's just that good.

Mason looks at Tom and there's a flurry of whispers between them before they turn to me and stare. "Young man, I'm not sure I agree with your business sense, but I admire it. I understand wanting to win fair and square, but while you're playing clean, someone else is always playing dirty."

I nod my head. "Agreed. But I'm the one who gets to sleep with a clear conscience every night."

"Tom, go get him the numbers."

What in the fuck did I just do?

Chapter Eighteen

Harper

"What in the hell was going on in there?" It's my first thought as Ryder emerges almost an hour later from the conference room. He looks frazzled and tired as he lifts his glasses and rubs his eyes.

Exactly like how I felt out here pacing the halls, wondering if they'd awarded him the job, concluded they had, and ready to figure out my next step for a job since I'd fallen short for Wade and Meteor. But the look on his face tells me differently. It's not one of jubilation but is rather pensive and stressed.

"Just a lot of questions," he murmurs and yet he doesn't look me in the eye for more than a second or two before glancing around at the others staring at him and wondering why he was in there so long.

"Can we have everyone in the conference room, please," Mason requests, snapping everyone's attention off of Ryder and to him. The room fills with the sound of shuffling and the tension is palpable as people move toward the room, and yet I stand and hold Ryder's eyes. Try to figure out what they are telling me without telling me. There's a quiet sadness there with a hint of something more…that I just can't read and before I can look too deeply, he lifts his eyebrows in *shall we.*

He follows behind me as we walk into the conference room, and I hate that all I feel is a sense of discord when this morning there was so much more between us.

I should be smiling. I'm coming down from the high of numerous bouts of incredible sex with a hot guy.

I should be excited. I'm back in the game after two years, doing what I love to do, and I'll find out if my gamble in telling Wade I'd get the contract in exchange for the Director of Development position will pay off.

I should be second-guessing myself why I'm not either of the above, and yet I'm doing neither. Instead I just want that feeling back from this morning when I was ready to conquer the world instead of wondering if I'm about to lose a piece of it.

I exhale an unsteady breath and glance over to Ryder, who's looking straight ahead at Mason. But his knee is jogging up and down and that tells me he's just as nervous as I am.

"I'd like to thank you all for your hard work in completing your bid packages. We had a set of unusual circumstances come to light when we were in the process of awarding the bid." Murmuring begins throughout the room and I can feel the trepidation and unease in the air as we all look to each other wondering what Mason means by the comment. "Due to these circumstances, we've made a slight change to the project."

Ryder's knee jogs harder.

My fingers wring together.

"Phase One has been awarded to R Squared Management."

Ryder's sharp inhale of air is audible just before the room breaks out in chatter as heads nod and thumbs-up are given his way.

I glance over to him and he smiles softly at me. Something is off with him; I'm not sure what. I'm thrilled for him. And at the same time am more than disappointed because I just failed Wade. And myself.

Back to square one with a pocketful of hope and a heart full of determination.

"And phase 2," Mason says, snapping the room to attention

when we thought the awarding was already over. "Phase 2 has been awarded to Meteor Development."

It's my gasp I hear this time. It's my disbelief that clouds everything else I hear around me as I try to wrap my head around what's going on.

I don't understand it.

But I'll take it.

My heart is pounding through the confusion; my eyes are fighting back the tears stinging in my throat.

My doubt whether I lost my touch vanishes.

Our table is swarmed with well wishes from our disappointed but considerate colleagues. And it's only when they leave the room to begin to clean up their desks that I am able to turn and look over to Ryder.

He's sitting facing me, elbow on the table, fingers playing with that beard of his, eyes full of emotion.

"Congratulations," he says softly, almost as if he wants to absorb the moment in silence a bit longer.

And so I let him. With my eyes on his. With our smiles wide.

Until I can't stand it any more.

"What in the hell happened in there, Ryder?"

"It's a long story. I'll tell you about it later."

"So this means we kind of get to work together for once. Not against each other. However are we going to handle that?" The thought strikes me as I speak and makes me smile even wider.

He leans forward and lowers his voice. "Considering your panties are currently renting space in my jacket pocket, I can think of a lot of ways we can handle it."

I laugh. "Good thing you came in early then and found them."

"*You have no idea.*" And for some reason, I know he's talking about more than just finding my panties. His face becomes serious for a moment, eyes flicking over to where Mason and another guy are speaking, before looking back to mine and filling with mischief. "I think we need to set some ground rules right off the bat though."

"Seriously?"

"Yes." His smile widens. "Since we both won, does that mean

we both get reward sex?"

"Does that mean double the orgasms?" My body is already reacting to the thought. The sweet rivalry between us just became a whole lot sweeter.

"Yes. It does." He leans in close, the heat of his breath tickling my ear. "And it also means double the *beard burn.*"

Sign up for the 1001 Dark Nights Newsletter
and be entered to win a Tiffany Key necklace.

There's a contest every month!

Go to www.1001DarkNights.com to subscribe.

As a bonus, all subscribers will receive a free
1001 Dark Nights story
The First Night
by Lexi Blake & M.J. Rose

Turn the page for a full list of the
1001 Dark Nights fabulous novellas...

Discover 1001 Dark Nights Collection Four

Go to www.1001DarkNights.com for more information.

ROCK CHICK REAWAKENING by Kristen Ashley
A Rock Chick Novella

ADORING INK by Carrie Ann Ryan
A Montgomery Ink Novella

SWEET RIVALRY by K. Bromberg

SHADE'S LADY by Joanna Wylde
A Reapers MC Novella

RAZR by Larissa Ione
A Demonica Underworld Novella

ARRANGED by Lexi Blake
A Masters and Mercenaries Novella

TANGLED by Rebecca Zanetti
A Dark Protectors Novella

HOLD ME by J. Kenner
A Stark Ever After Novella

SOMEHOW, SOME WAY by Jennifer Probst
A Billionaire Builders Novella

TOO CLOSE TO CALL by Tessa Bailey
A Romancing the Clarksons Novella

HUNTED by Elisabeth Naughton
An Eternal Guardians Novella

EYES ON YOU by Laura Kaye
A Blasphemy Novella

BLADE by Alexandra Ivy/Laura Wright
A Bayou Heat Novella

DRAGON BURN by Donna Grant
A Dark Kings Novella

TRIPPED OUT by Lorelei James
A Blacktop Cowboys® Novella

STUD FINDER by Lauren Blakely

MIDNIGHT UNLEASHED by Lara Adrian
A Midnight Breed Novella

HALLOW BE THE HAUNT by Heather Graham
A Krewe of Hunters Novella

DIRTY FILTHY FIX by Laurelin Paige
A Fixed Novella

THE BED MATE by Kendall Ryan
A Room Mate Novella

NIGHT GAMES by CD Reiss
A Games Novella

NO RESERVATIONS by Kristen Proby
A Fusion Novella

DAWN OF SURRENDER by Liliana Hart
A MacKenzie Family Novella

Discover 1001 Dark Nights Collection One

Go to www.1001DarkNights.com for more information.

FOREVER WICKED by Shayla Black
CRIMSON TWILIGHT by Heather Graham
CAPTURED IN SURRENDER by Liliana Hart
SILENT BITE: A SCANGUARDS WEDDING by Tina Folsom
DUNGEON GAMES by Lexi Blake
AZAGOTH by Larissa Ione
NEED YOU NOW by Lisa Renee Jones
SHOW ME, BABY by Cherise Sinclair
ROPED IN by Lorelei James
TEMPTED BY MIDNIGHT by Lara Adrian
THE FLAME by Christopher Rice
CARESS OF DARKNESS by Julie Kenner

Also from 1001 Dark Nights

TAME ME by J. Kenner

Discover 1001 Dark Nights Collection Two

Go to www.1001DarkNights.com for more information.

WICKED WOLF by Carrie Ann Ryan
WHEN IRISH EYES ARE HAUNTING by Heather Graham
EASY WITH YOU by Kristen Proby
MASTER OF FREEDOM by Cherise Sinclair
CARESS OF PLEASURE by Julie Kenner
ADORED by Lexi Blake
HADES by Larissa Ione
RAVAGED by Elisabeth Naughton
DREAM OF YOU by Jennifer L. Armentrout
STRIPPED DOWN by Lorelei James
RAGE/KILLIAN by Alexandra Ivy/Laura Wright
DRAGON KING by Donna Grant
PURE WICKED by Shayla Black
HARD AS STEEL by Laura Kaye
STROKE OF MIDNIGHT by Lara Adrian
ALL HALLOWS EVE by Heather Graham
KISS THE FLAME by Christopher Rice
DARING HER LOVE by Melissa Foster
TEASED by Rebecca Zanetti
THE PROMISE OF SURRENDER by Liliana Hart

Also from 1001 Dark Nights

THE SURRENDER GATE By Christopher Rice
SERVICING THE TARGET By Cherise Sinclair

Discover 1001 Dark Nights Collection Three

Go to www.1001DarkNights.com for more information.

About K. Bromberg

New York Times Bestselling author K. Bromberg writes contemporary novels that contain a mixture of sweet, emotional, a whole lot of sexy, and a little bit of real. She likes to write strong heroines, and damaged heroes who we love to hate and hate to love.

She's a mixture of most of her female characters: sassy, intelligent, stubborn, reserved, outgoing, driven, emotional, strong, and wears her heart on her sleeve. All of which she displays daily with her family and friends where she lives in Southern California.

In 2013, K. Bromberg decided her part time job in accounting wasn't cutting it and decided to try her hand at this writing thing. Since then she has written eleven novels, landing over half of them on the New York's Time Bestseller's list and all but one of them on the USA Today's bestseller list. She's also a Wall Street Journal bestseller and an Amazon pick for best romance of 2013.

Her most notable series has been the Driven Series, its spin-off novels, and her standalone novel Sweet Cheeks.

Her plans for 2017 include a novella titled Sweet Rivalry, a sports romance duet (The Player (4/17), The Catch (July)) and the Everyday Heroes series (3 books: Cuffed, Combust, and Cockpit).

She loves to hear from her readers so make sure you check her out on social media or sign up for her newsletter.

The Player

By K. Bromberg

Coming April 17, 2017

Baseball has never been sexier in an all-new novel by *New York Times Bestselling Author,* **K. Bromberg.**

Easton Wylder is baseball royalty. The game is his life. His passion. *His everything.*

So, when an injury threatens to end Easton's season early, the team calls in renowned physical therapist, Doc Dalton, to oversee his recovery. Except it's not Doc who greets Easton for his first session, but rather, his daughter, Scout. She may be feisty, athletic, defiant, and gorgeous, but Easton is left questioning whether she has what it takes to help him.

Scout Dalton's out to prove a female can handle the pressure of running the physical therapy regimen of an MLB club. And that proof comes in the form of getting phenom Easton Wylder back on the field. But getting him healthy means being hands-on.

And with a man as irresistible as Easton, being hands-on can only lead to one thing, *trouble.* Because the more she touches him, the more she wants him, and *she can't want him.* Not when it's her job to maintain the club's best interest, in regards to whether he's ready to play.

But when sparks fly and fine lines are crossed, can they withstand the heat, or is one of them bound to get burned?

* * * *

Scout

Each thump of Easton's stride on the treadmill irritates me more than the last.

Every grunt of exertion adds to it.

And then there's the beep. The one that tells me his thirty minutes of high intensity running is complete, and now it's my turn to complete the session.

Lucky me.

I'm irritable. Pissed off. And I'm not sure if my current mood stems from exhaustion after spending too many hours last night Googling Easton Wylder or that it seems he was doing the same about me.

"So are you actually going to touch my arm today, or are you only good for telling me *treadmill, thirty minutes, level ten?* If you wanted to avoid me, then maybe you should call in sick for the next few months." Sarcasm drips from his voice. His obvious disdain for me, more than evident, and that even keel I thought we might have found yesterday, seemingly nonexistent.

I need to turn around, to face him, but I stall. The images from Google last night are seared in my mind. The charity calendar pictures where he's wearing nothing but a strategically placed baseball glove. The ESPN body issue where he's batting—naked—the twist of his legs hiding his package. The three-piece suit at the ESPYs. All of them are there, floating around, reminding me how all those hard lines and toned edges look like in person.

And it would take a dead woman to not be affected by him.

So, I steel myself for the visceral impact of looking at him—hot, sweaty, relaxed—but it doesn't help when I turn around. I'm not sure anything could. Because even in his sweat-dampened T-shirt, he's still breathtakingly handsome with his mixture of All-American and rugged outdoorsman. He still exudes that tinge of arrogance. And the odd thing is, today, when I look at him, after I've stared at pictures of him for hours last night, somehow the arrogance adds to his appeal.

And then he smirks, and I shake my head and question my

own sanity.

"So you actually want me to look at your arm? You mean you'll trust me with it? And here I was under the impression you thought I was just a *trophy* trainer."

"Come again?" he chuckles.

Time to clear the air between us. Being handsome doesn't override being an asshole. "You know, *trophy trainer*—someone good for you to look at, but incapable of much else."

"If the shoe fits." He shrugs.

I take a step closer to him, his sarcastic comeback igniting the embers of my temper he lit yesterday. "Don't be a jerk. If you want to find out if I'm qualified for the job—capable of getting you back in top form—then *you ask me* for my credentials. You want a resume? You want references? I'd be glad to hand you a list of them, so don't go snooping around, making phone calls, and questioning everything about me without talking to me first. *Got it?*"

Our eyes hold as he worries his bottom lip between his teeth to combat the smile he's fighting as he takes a step toward me. "You want me to take my rehab seriously, right? Then don't chastise me for making sure the person charged to do it is up to par and has the right experience. I don't trust my body with just anyone, let alone a rookie trainer still learning the ropes. *Got it?*"

"*Touché*," I murmur as we wage a visual war of defiance and misunderstanding. "We're wasting time. Let's get started."

Maybe if we begin I'll forget about the phone calls I'd received last night. The ones from previous clients and personal friends I'd rehabbed letting me know I was being vetted. I was glad for the friends letting me know, and pissed at being questioned.

I grab the ultrasound cart and wheel it toward the table, but he's still standing there like yesterday, still questioning me. Obviously, the point is not moot, but I shrug it off, knowing after my rebuke of him, he was bound to either respect me or test me, and by the current standoff, I'm guessing it will be the latter.

"Yes?" I finally ask when he doesn't budge.

"You wanna tell me where Doc is?"

"He's got a packed schedule on the East Coast right now. As

you know, injury happens without warning." I hold his gaze and hope he doesn't see through the lie.

"Uh-huh." He just nods, but I can tell he's not convinced. But there must be something in my eyes he sees—the something I'm trying desperately to keep together—that prevents him from digging deeper. *"He's the best there is."*

"Agreed."

"Shouldn't I be worried then?"

"About?" I prompt.

"If he's the best, then doesn't that mean you're second best?"

His remark serves its purpose and hits closer to home than I'd like, but it's his body, his career, and his right to ask.

"Second best to Doc Dalton isn't a bad place to be. I learned everything I know from the man. I assure you, he's the last person I want to let down, and therefore, you're the beneficiary of that fear . . . so. . ." I quirk my brows. *"Lucky you."*

"Lucky me," he murmurs but still doesn't move. "The problem is I still don't know shit about you, and yet you're standing there ready to work on my arm."

"What do you want to know?" I'm getting impatient. Another day, another round of bullshit and once again, time is wasting away. But at least he listened and is asking me and not snooping around.

"What were your stats in the Major Leagues?"

"What?"

"I asked your stats. Errors. On base percentage. Batting average. Fielding percentage. You know, statistics."

"I know what statistics are," I respond dryly.

"But if you've never played in the Majors, how is it you know how my arm's supposed to feel so that you can get it back to one hundred percent?"

He's neglecting the fact that no other trainer has played in the Major Leauges either . . . but I have a better way to shut him up. "Have you ever been a woman?"

"What?" It's his turn to be surprised by an unexpected question. "Of course not. I've got plenty of proof that I'm a man?"

I roll my eyes, half-expecting him to grab his crotch and equally relieved that he doesn't. "Well, if you've never been a woman, how is it you know how to please one in bed? How do you know if you're hitting the right spot? Getting her off?"

He fights back the bark of a laugh, but eventually lets it escape as he just shakes his head at me. "Touché," he repeats my words back to me.

"If you're going to bust my chops, Wylder, you should know that I can give as good as I get."

"Point taken. But since you're the one singlehandedly charged with busting my balls in rehab over the next three months, you've gotta admit, it was a valid question."

"It was," I concede, "but it's your job to talk to me, tell me how it feels, where it hurts, and when it feels good, so I can make it better." An unexpectedly shy smile slides on his lips when he gets the correlation between what I asked about how to please a woman and my answer.

"Just like sex."

"Perhaps." I smile; it's all I can do as heat flushes my cheeks and the room around us becomes too small for him and this innuendo-laced conversation. "Some men have all the tools in the world, but if they don't know how to use them, they're useless. It's the same with my job. You've gotta know how to use your skills, and I assure you, I do. So, if the I-don't-trust-you-because-you-have-a-vagina-card has been exhausted, can we get started?" I point to the table behind him as he chuckles, and then I begin to adjust the machine.

"You drive a hard bargain, *Kitty*." He sits down and pulls off his shirt, discarding it to right of him.

"You ain't seen nothing yet."

On behalf of 1001 Dark Nights,

Liz Berry and M.J. Rose would like to thank ~

Steve Berry
Doug Scofield
Kim Guidroz
Jillian Stein
InkSlinger PR
Dan Slater
Asha Hossain
Chris Graham
Pamela Jamison
Fedora Chen
Jessica Johns
Dylan Stockton
Richard Blake
BookTrib After Dark
and Simon Lipskar